ARLY'S RUN

Books by
Robert Newton Peck

A Day No Pigs Would Die
Path of Hunters
Millie's Boy
Soup
Fawn
Wild Cat
Bee Tree
Soup and Me
Hamilton
Hang for Treason
Rabbits and Redcoats
King of Kazoo
Trig
Last Sunday
The King's Iron
Patooie
Soup for President
Eagle Fur
Trig Sees Red
Basket Case
Hub
Mr. Little
Clunie
Soup's Drum
Secrets of Successful Fiction

Trig Goes Ape
Soup on Wheels
Justice Lion
Kirk's Law
Trig or Treat
Banjo
Soup in the Saddle
Fiction Is Folks
The Seminole Seed
Soup's Goat
Dukes
Spanish Hoof
Jo Silver
Soup on Ice
Soup on Fire
My Vermont
Hallapoosa
The Horse Hunters
Soup's Uncle
My Vermont II
Arly
Soup's Hoop
Higbee's Halloween
Little Soup's Hayride
Little Soup's Birthday

ARLY'S RUN

Robert Newton Peck

WALKER AND COMPANY
NEW YORK

First published in the United States of America in 1991
by Walker Publishing Company, Inc.

Published simultaneously in Canada by Thomas Allen & Son
Canada, Limited, Markham, Ontario

Library of Congress Cataloging-in-Publication Data
Peck, Robert Newton.
        Arly's run/Robert Newton Peck.
            p.   cm.
        Summary: Arly, an orphan in search of a home and a family, escapes from a brutal migrant labor camp, joins a traveling religious show, and battles a devastating Florida hurricane.
        ISBN 0-8027-8120-9
        [1. Orphans—Fiction.   2. Migrant labor—Fiction.   3. Hurricanes—Fiction.   4. Florida—Fiction.]   I. Title.
        PZ7.P339As   1991
[Fic]—dc20   91-23606
                                                                              CIP
                                                                              AC

Printed in the United States of America

10 9 8 7 6 5 4 3 2 1

DEDICATION

Robins and geese migrate.

So do caribou, and whales.

There is also migratory humanity. Our planet abounds with traveling tribes: Gypsies. Tent people. Nomads. Kurds.

Here in Florida, they are migrant workers. Field hands. Pickers. Without them, there would be no produce in supermarkets. No greengrocers or fruit stands. No salad bars.

To most things, there's a top and a bottom.

Humanity's base is stoop labor. It has always existed and always will. You and I are too fortunate to choose harvesting as a profession. Americans (white, brown, or black) will not chop sugarcane. Jamaicans will.

To harvest is to move. Crop to crop, state to state, and season by season. Comparing apples to oranges, both, when ripe, demand a homeless hand.

Because of days under sun, nights in shacks, and many a body louse lent to me by others, I have often met the Florida migrant on his turf. Worked, fought, gambled, eaten, drunk cheap wine and petrol, slept (and scratched) with the best of them.

And the worst.

Having no desire to change them, only to accept

them, I allowed *them* to inform *me*. Most of all, I was touched by their children. I discovered that friendship is based on working with . . . not talking to.

Research is merely getting dirty, hot, tired . . . among those who do the same for a lifetime.

Thus, my dedication is a tribute to their dedication, to eight people, who helped promote an author to a man:

Tico Taco	Movement
Big Tree Fellow	P. Man
Fat Rat	Zarbadio
DuCoste	No Eye

To these, and to each and every field hand whose spine is bent from labor, weather, and poverty . . . but who can still smile . . . I dedicate *Arly's Run*.

ARLY'S RUN

PROLOGUE

AFRICA

August 1928

Zakoolu was a wrinkled man with black skin, and very white hair, who had lived a long time, outdoors, and had learned many a lesson.

To live, he caught fish.

He worked unafraid, yet respectfully, between two giants. Above one and beneath the other. Their size was too vast for Zakoolu to imagine, and he suspected that these giants were unaware that he (a speck of life) existed. He only knew their names:

Sea and *sky.*

At every dawn, wearing nothing except a crude hat of woven palm stems, Zakoolu carried a mast and sail to his little boat; then sailed westward, away from the early sun, so far that he could no longer see the green treetops of home.

He was alone with two giants.

His friends.

One giant fed him fish. The other supplied wind to feed his hungry sail. When the giants were at peace, both his belly and his sail were filled.

The sky was male, like himself, for its wind carried seeds and pollen dust. The ocean, however, was a warm, wet woman who bore many fruits of fish, to eat raw. He knew the sky was male because he, Zakoolu, could see all of it. A man knows all of another man. But, beneath his bobbing boat lay a female sea, of which he saw only the surface. No man could know the depths of a woman.

A man was outside.

A woman, inside.

Hardly ever did the two giants quarrel. But sometimes they would mate, to produce a violent offspring composed of wind and water. An unruly whelp that caused the sea and sky to battle one another as their weather bud grew, and grew, to conquer all it touched.

Squinting, he saw it happening again.

Earlier, the gulls had seen it, or sensed it. They were shrieking, no longer hunting for fish, but flying, with no clear purpose.

The gulls knew.

After years of calm, another purple pup was being conceived, rising in birth from sea to sky, wildly whirling in its waltz.

He watched until his neck ached.

Luckily for Zakoolu, the storm wasn't near.

Nevertheless, by tiller and rudder, he silently pointed his bow southward, then eastward, away from the storm. Beneath him, a foaming ocean now raged and roared its fury.

Rain fell. Moisture rose.

Above, the devil child grew larger, as do all children, and headed west. And it could, Zakoolu knew,

2

destroy anything in its path. Tantrums such as this, the old fisher had observed, often turned animals and people as crazy as the turbulent sky. And their floods whipped dogs to climb trees.

As the storm churned farther and farther from the West African shore, Zakoolu wondered where it would go.

He knew nothing of a distant place called Florida, thousands of miles to the west, or a lake that a foreign tribe had named Okeechobee.

Not even a wise, aging fisherman could foretell the might of this young assassin now being spawned by giants. One that was destined to swell to a monster of one million cubic miles. Zakoolu only knew the evil one by name. An ancient name.

Trembling, he whispered the word.

"Hurakan."

CHAPTER 1

1927

The night thickened.

Sitting on the damp stern seat of Brother Smith's sculler boat, I watched the big gray-haired colored man rowing the two of us toward the deeper waters of Lake Okeechobee.

I tried not to cry.

All I could think of was that I, Arly Poole, was final escaping from dirty old Jailtown, Florida.

Making off for keeps. The field boss, Mr. Roscoe Broda, and his guns and blood-dogs wouldn't be driving me into no gator swamp. He'd not drag me back to Shack Row with his rope burning me fearful. He done it once, over cactus, through mud and the pricker palmetto. The rope burns had cut me deep enough to leave scars. Tonight, I'd be the only runaway field picker or cane chopper who wouldn't git kicked or whipped or fist-beaten.

I was free.

Even though all I knowed is that I'm a orphan, a inch taller than half-growed, a picker's son, leaving Jailtown and going to Moore Haven to start a new life, I couldn't help shooting a in-the-dark smile at Brother.

He was barefoot, like me. His feet looked near three times the size of mine. Maybe even four.

As he leaned forward, there was moonlight enough to see his big black hands working the oar handles.

He smiled back.

"You go free, Arly Poole."

Other than Brother Smith's deep voice, there was very few sounds, merely the whine of the oarlocks and the dipping of the blades breaking the surface of Okeechobee. At every stroke, Brother Smith would grunt; and beneath me, I could feel the thrust of his might, pulling the boat forward to a place I didn't know.

Moore Haven.

Miss Hoe said I'd still live in Florida, and only a few miles away. Far enough. All I'd ever knowed was Jailtown, owned by Captain Genesis Tant. He own the sugarmill, produce fields, the store, the judge and the jail. Captain own Shack Row where my mama died when I got born. And where my daddy died of sunburnt labor. He'd be a picker almost all of his life.

The night we buried Dan Poole, my daddy, Brother Smith come to our shack to say words over him, and read from his Bible. Weren't even one preacher in Jailtown. Yet everybody, be they white (like us) or colored, needed Brother Smith to help bury their departed.

Nobody had to say it.

We all knowed that Brother lived closer to God than all the rest of us dirties, whether we was black or white. Even the people who wore *shoes* knowed of Brother Smith; and how, a long number of years back, he'd pulled the Captain's only child, Miss Liddy, up from the bottom waters of Okeechobee so she'd survive.

Not a living soul in Jailtown dare to trespass on Brother; including the field boss, Roscoe Broda, with his big horse, his whip, and his catching rope.

Brother Smith strained.

He weren't no longer young. Maybe to row a sculler boat from Jailtown south to Moore Haven would be too heavy for him to handle. One way, it was miles. And then he would have to row back to Jailtown.

"Brother," I whispered in the night, "if'n your backbone gets tired, or cramps up into a misery, I can row, to spell you."

Without missing an oar stroke, he shook his head.

I felt safe along with Brother. Everybody did. Even though I didn't have no idea of how God looked like, I figured He certain had to favor Brother Smith. I just wager that God was big and black and gentle kind, and just as wise as Brother.

He quit rowing.

I couldn't hear no more squeaking of the oarlocks as the pivot pegs turned in their sockets.

"Hush," whispered Brother.

Over his beefy shoulder, I couldn't see to make out a doggone thing. Only the night. Both of Brother's oar blades now hovered over the water, dripping drops, making a series of little circles that we floated by, one by each, as I saw them grow.

"What it's be?" I asked Brother Smith, without making any sound at all.

Hunching his giant shoulders up, then down, he told me that he didn't rightful know. Yet, by the way Brother Smith now cupped a hand to his ear, possible there was trouble ahead of us, off in the mist beyond the prow of our sculler.

Breathing, I could smell fish.

Brother was a catfisher on Okeechobee. He'd catch enough to feed himself and then divvy out a supper to several of the worst-off in Darky Town. He also had give catfish and bass to some of the good whites, like us two Pooles, before Papa die.

"Hold quiet," Brother Smith whispered.

Listening, I could've swore I'd heared something, a human voice. And now, my ears picked up a second voice. Two men, ahead of us in the lake fog.

No kicker engine.

They must've been in a oar boat.

Like us.

Leaning back, Brother Smith pulled his oars to a rest, so's I could hold the wet blades and settle 'em quiet in the stern. He didn't fix to leave the oar blades to thump against the hull. We just drifted. Turning his body around, Brother ducked down to look ahead, over our prow.

Common sense warn me not to ask Brother if he could see anything, or anybody. His hand was hushing me to still. "The night," Brother Smith had once told Huff Cooter and me, "has a foolish mouth but a wise ear."

Ahead, I hear oars splashing.

Somebody be rowing.

It near to stopped my heart. Because I was afeared they might be Mr. Roscoe Broda's crew. His catcher men, the ones that took after people who tried to run away from Shack Row, back in Jailtown. All us pickers was nothing more than *rented slaves,* or so Miss Hoe had told Huff and me. Miss Binnie Hoe had been our schoolteacher, the first (and only one) in Jailtown. It'd been Miss Hoe who'd planned my getaway tonight, and arranged for me soon to live with new people.

Mr. and Mrs. Alfred Bonner.

Thinking about it, my fingers snuck inside my shirt (actual it was Mrs. Newell's dead husband's shirt) to touch the letter, the one that'd tell me where to go, once Brother Smith row me to Moore Haven.

I could feel it.

And hear the paper crackle.

That letter was my ticket to freedom, according to what Mrs. Newell and Miss Binnie Hoe had told me. Because the new people, in Moore Haven, were cousins to Mrs. Newell, who run Newell's Boarding House in Jailtown, where Miss Hoe had herself a upstairs room.

I'd slept there one time. In a room.

Instead of a straw tick, like Papa and me rested on in Shack Row, the Mrs. Newell place had two white cloths, big ones, on the bed, and you'd sleep in between. Cleaner than Sunday.

Mrs. Newell's didn't smell like Shack Row. It didn't have no picker stink, and no sweaty cane-crusher smell to it neither, no sir. Smelled sort of the way Heaven ought.

Papa was up there yonder.

In shade.

Before I'd left Jailtown, I'd poured maybe half a handful of his grave dirt into the chest pocket of my new grow-into shirt, the one wore by the dead Mr. Elbert Newell. The tip of my finger now touched the dirt, to be sure it was still there. Safe and snug. It was all I could take with me of my daddy.

My teacher, Miss Binnie Hoe, actual come to Shack Row, and she called my daddy *Mr.* Poole, like him and me was somebody.

Mr. Dan Poole, a picker.

I couldn't seem to make myself quit my remembering. 'Twas all sort of a big book in my mind, with pictures to every page. As the pages kept turning, faster and faster, the little pictures refused to stay separate. They all joined like a crazy quilt.

Holding my breath, I now could see the other boat. It was cutting across our bow, splashing through the mist. No more than six or seven oar lengths in front of us.

Its two men kept talking. One said something about *jugs* and his partner mentioned *money*.

Miss Hoe had tried to explain Prohibition, and that it was illegal to make, transport, or sell any flavor of strong spirits. Why? I couldn't understand.

After the boat passed us, we still held quiet for a long time, at least a hundred breaths. Brother Smith leaned close to me, after a while, and spoke.

"Rummers," he whispered, "would kill for a cork."

CHAPTER 2

It rained.

The sculler boat had no roof. From under his middle seat, Brother Smith pull a small sheet of tarp, and make a tent to cover me.

Brother sat in the downpour, total wet, a big hand protecting his eyes as he kept a lookout.

The rain continue, very hard.

Brother Smith laugh. "Those poor old rum-runner boys," he said, "is getting twice as wet. Because" —he slapped his soaking thigh—"they's two of them bootleggers and only one of me."

It slowly let up, and final stop.

Using a couple of bailer cans, we scoop up most of the water and tossed it over the side. When, by mistake, I clank my can against the boat's wooden gunwale, my big friend shook his head at me, and begged me to hush quiet.

"Arly," he whispered, "sharp metal sound'll travel a ways over water. We don't seek no trouble from the whiskey ginks. Does we?"

"No," I breathed.

After waiting a bit more, Brother Smith push the oar handles down, and gently swing both blades into the water, behind him, in a ready position. Taking a deep gulp of wet night air, Brother pull, and we moved.

He rowed and he rowed.

Folding the tarpaulin, I tucked the wet side in, to form a pillow. My eyes sagged, and my head rested down. I didn't rightly intend to sleep. It just come sneaking up. My eyes close and I dream of Jailtown, and a girl I had feelings about, Essie May Cooter. I could vision her at the Lucky Leg Social Palace, working for the boss-lady there, Miss Angel Free. She weren't much more'n fourteen. The life she'd chose wouldn't be a picnic, socializing the dredger toughs and the poker dandies.

Miss Angel had promise Essie that she knowed a special doctor that would operate, so Essie May wouldn't git herself in a family way. She wouldn't be like fat Addie, her mama, with a litter of five and no husband.

"Essie," I mumbled. "I'll come back for you, Essie May Cooter. You won't rot your life away in a . . . a social parlor."

My body flinched.

Opening my eyes with a start, I saw Brother Smith. He was standing on the middle seat and looking out through the misty night in all directions, turning his head this way and thataway, and squinting.

"Are we lost?" I asked.

The wind had come up, and I could feel our sculler drifting. It didn't have a sail, or a rudder; it got driven by nothing except the strong of a nice old man.

"No, child, we ain't lost. We's on Okeechobee."

His voice sort of told me that we was.

I felt scared.

"Can you swim, Brother?"

He nodded. "Enough to grab a float."

"Well," I told him, "I can't."

"Stick to the boat," he order me. "No matter what, Arly boy, best you grab a purchase on your stern gunwale, and don't leave go. Hear?"

"I hear."

Turning my head to one side, then to the other, old Okeechobee looked black and deep and evil, like it could suck somebody under to where they'd be no air. No life.

"Please sit down," I said.

"You worry?"

"Yes, account you'll fall yourself in. And you become Miss Liddy Tant, going down, and I won't be able to fish you out again, like you done for her, years back."

"Who told you?"

"Everybody in Jailtown know the whole entire story. How you save the Captain's only child, Miss Liddy, years and years and years back ago, when Miss Liddy Tant weren't no more than a bug."

Brother Smith sat.

"It's true." He took a extra breath. "But I didn't save that little doll of a girl because she be Captain's daughter. I save her in spite of. She about drowning. Down below, in the dark deeps of Okeechobee, all she'd become would be just one more dead white. But then the Lord commanded me to do a action. At the time, Arly Poole, I didn't know that the drowning child be a Tant. Only a child, Arly . . . a little child in need."

"What are you telling me, that you hated all white people, like us Pooles?"

Brother Smith nodded. "I didn't like hardly nobody, colored or white, or even a in-between. Oh, I hated. Arly, I wanted to make my hand into a fist, and I was fixing to strike every face I'd see. Reckon I hate the white faces worst. Mr. Roscoe Broda weren't come to Jailtown back in those days. Not yet. Instead, the field boss was another whitey, name of Lundee Yoder."

"Was he mean, like Broda?"

"Meaner. Mr. Yoder would easily make Mr. Broda appear to be first cousin to the Angel Gabriel."

"How mean was he, Brother? Nobody alive is meaner than Mr. Roscoe Broda. How mean? I want to know."

Before giving me an answer, Brother Smith look at the sky. "We wait . . . until the fog lifts and I can locate stars." He sit to the middle sculler seat. "So I shall tell you, Arly Poole."

I held patient.

Brother Smith told his story.

"Years back, I was young and strong, and I could work a turpentine mill alongside of any big nigger alive. Had me a mama, a good woman, and a young sister whose name was Rubee . . . Rubee Louise Smith. We call her Rubee Lou."

"Where is Rubee right now?"

"She clean gone." Again he looked at the heavens. "Up in a good yonder, with our Lord." He looked at me again. "But I be telling you about Mr. Lundee Yoder." Brother hauled in a breath. "Now that gent was a sorry white. There's some sorry coloreds, too. Sorry whites. And Mr. Yoder certain fit to be one."

"What'd he do?"

"I was a young'n. Working at the turpentine mill for five cents a day. Fifty year ago, that be a respectable pay for black work." He paused. "We took ourselfs a noontime, to eat, to chew a little chatter bone . . . that's a colored word for talk . . . and to feed a couple of fatback scraps to a dog. Nobody knowed this dog's proper name. Or his owner. He just was a friendly little critter who'd chum around us turpers, to beg eats."

"What happened?"

"The back-to-work whistle blowed. Most of the boys, all except me, jumped up to go back to the still."

"I don't know about turpentine."

Brother hunkered down in the boat, to lean back against the seat, like he felt like storytelling.

"Turp comes from tall trees. Two kinds. Longleaf pine and slash pine. We cut the bark off and the gummy sap runs and collects in little cups. They empty into big buckets. Sap gits boiled. Then the oil of turpentine gits put up in barrels, to make paint, melt rubber, and help to form a camphor. Turp makes a medicine, too."

I looked at him.

"Brother, how come you got so learny and all? You know so much that it's right near to spooky."

Brother Smith laughed.

"Then, if I be so smarty, how come I'm lost?"

I felt sweaty, and sudden.

"But you said—"

Brother held up a easy hand. "Arly, you wait until the stars do shine, and point us the way. Then we'll go. Right now, we do best to stay patient and trust Jesus."

He was silent for a spell. Then he speak.

"Like I said, the back-to-work whistle blowed, and the turpers all hop on work. Except me. I stay behind to feed a pet dog. But I didn't see nobody come up behind me. Or hear. And then sudden, while I be feeding a scrap to a nice little animal, a ax handle slash through the air, just missing my ear, and crack the dog's head."

I couldn't breathe.

"Was it . . . ?"

"Yes, my child, it was Mr. Lundee Yoder. He'd

smashed the skull of the only little pooch we have for a pet. Right near me, there be a ax handle, with a double-bit blade on the business end. And I felt my hand reach out to fetch me that ax, to even a score . . . to put a end to Yoder."

"Did you?"

Brother Smith let out a sigh.

"No. It'd be wrong. Somewhere, by somebody, the killing had to stop, instead of double. If'n I struck Mr. Lundee Yoder, I'd hanged under a tree from a rope. In Florida, no nigger's allowed to cut down a white. Ought to be such for all people." He held up a hand. "Don't git me wrong. And, young Arly, please don't you ever mix up right and wrong, good or bad, or colored or white."

"I don't understand."

Brother Smith then explain it for me.

"All good peoples got a clean color inside."

CHAPTER 3

Brother Smith was rowing again.
The fog had melted off, or blowed away, but there weren't nary a signal of a morning sun.

I'd dozed off. With my eyes now open, my backbone felt more'n a mite stiff from the shape I'd curled myself into on the hard stern seat. There was a crick in my neck like I'd got hanged.

Stars be out. A few.

But a night breeze had kicked up, turning fierce, and our sculler was shipping water. More with every wave. We bailed instead of rowed, yet Brother and I couldn't keep up with the stronger waves splashing over the gunwales. Brother Smith was a very large man, so the boat already sat low in the water.

"Bail quick, Arly."

We both tried. Yet our bailer cans couldn't do it. The sculler kept filling. As the inside water become deeper and deeper, Okeechobee rolling rougher by the second, I could read the worry on Brother Smith's face. The wind growed.

"Boy, we about to swamp."

Right after he said it, the sculler boat started to sink. It just sunk below us, into the deep. Yanking a oar from its locks, Brother shoved it under both my arms and across my chest. Only my face was out of water.

The boat had flipped over.

It float now, bottom up. My fingernails clawed at its slimy hull that was coated with scum.

I could see Brother Smith fighting the water, trying to keep hisself afloat. For his weight, the other oar didn't seem to be enough. His breathing was nothing except a wet gasp after another. A big black hand pointed me to somewhere in the night. In the distance, I spotted a pinpoint of flickering light.

Brother tried to say words, yet all I heard was a watery, gurgling sound. My old friend had rowed too long, too hard, and he couldn't seem to keep his face above water. His hat had floated away. All I could see was his white, woolly hair at the surface. Sinking.

No face. And no hands.

A bigger wave hit us, with force, and I was spewing up water. Looking around, I couldn't see him no more.

"Brother . . . Brother Smith!"

He was gone.

Kicking my feet as hard as I could, I kept on searching for him, calling out his name, between spits.

"Brother . . . Brother . . . Brother Smith."

The big deep voice never answered. And I couldn't see his gentle smile or the shining of God in his eyes.

He was gone.

Okeechobee had drag him under.

All I was wearing was a shirt and pants, a gift from Mrs. Newell. They'd once belonged to her dead husband. I had my important letter inside my shirt, and it probable was total soaked.

"Brother . . ."

My voice was wet, alone, and scared. I felt so heavy. Something was weighing me down. Two things, like lead sinkers. Somehow I managed to loosen my shirt and spill them out. Two books. I knowed they was important, but I couldn't recall why. My cookies were gone. So was my bundle of extra clothes. There was just a wet shirt, wet pants, an oar, and Arly Poole.

I kept up the kicking.

The oar weren't exactly floating, but it weren't yet sinking, and I kept both my arms over it, the way Brother Smith had done for me.

"Brother . . ."

It was like God was dead. My mind kept on saying his name, again and again. He couldn't be dead, not Brother Smith. Who'd say Bible words over his body? Where was he? Under me somewhere, in the deep of Okeechobee.

I kicked.

My legs start to tell me that maybe they weren't fixing to kick too much longer, or many more times. Good thing I didn't have on no shoes. People, so folks claimed, couldn't never swim in shoes.

Never, not a one time in my whole entire life, had I ever put even one shoe to my feet.

I'd never trusted *shoe people*.

"I ain't no shoe people," I spat into the water, speaking to nobody, and for no reason.

When a person drowns, he sort of goes crazy.

Leastwise, this is what I'd usual heared back in Jailtown. Right now, I didn't know a doggone thing for certain, except that I was away out over the deeps of Okeechobee and hadn't learnt how to swim. And that Brother Smith had left me alone.

"Brother?"

I tried one final time to call out his name, and maybe git back a answer. No such luck.

My mind wanted to yell out "Miss Hoe" too.

Maybe I'd not never see Miss Hoe again. She would feel awful bad when she learn about Brother Smith sinking into the drink.

"Miss Hoe . . . I'm sorry that Brother Smith had to die, just to deliver me to the Moore Haven place."

Keep kicking, I order myself.

Keep your legs and feet going, you dumb Arly Poole, and fix your sights on that little light up ahead. It was *shore*. Whether or not it'd be Moore Haven, I didn't rightly care, as long as it was dry land, and morning.

I kicked.

Not all the time, because I often had to quit for a resting, to cough out some Okeechobee. During my rests, I'd search my head around, one way and then another, hoping that I might catch me a glance at Brother's face.

Nobody.

No sign of his sculler boat.

Perhaps it was only my dreaming, or that I'd turned water crazy and fixing to drown, but the light be growing. Getting bigger. And look brighter. The notice of it made me work my legs again, harder, and faster, so eventual I might just git to a shore place.

It'd be Moore Haven.

I just knowed.

Under me, the toes of my right foot touched something. I wanted to yell for help. It happen again. Felt softy, like some sort of a seaweed. Huff Cooter claimed there was a strangle weed in Okeechobee, and it would grab ahold of a swimmer's feet and legs, then yank him under, to drown.

Both my feet was churning into the weedy stuff now, and I figured it just had to be strangle weed.

To pull me under.

To drown.

To die.

Right now I was kicking worse'n a crazy person, kicking hard and fast, and trying to claw my way toward the light.

My oar slip loose.

Reaching, my hand made a desperate grab for it, and missed. All I took a grip on was Okeechobee. And some weeds. As my head sunk under the surface, I couldn't see that oar. Not nowhere. But, before my head come up again, to cough out, my foot hit something hard beneath it, and I pushed up with my leg.

I did it all again.

Underneath, there was something half-solid, like mud. Or muck. Leastwise, it weren't all water.

I knowed what it was.

Land!

Above me, the light was a single bulb on a pole, and it now seemed to be higher in the air. And much closer. With every muddy step, and each push, I was coughing and fighting my way to shore. And I didn't even think about my losing the oar, because I didn't need it anymore.

Not now.

I'd made it.

The water was below my chin, working lower, and the solid stuff under my bare feet was feeling a lot firmer.

I was walking.

Well, not really walking just yet, but I sure was walking. My foot stepped on something sharp; it cut into me like a busted bottle, and really hurt like all fury, yet I didn't matter it that much. It beat water.

I'd fought Okeechobee.

And won.

Breathing hard, I looked back toward the lake, seeing only a large body of water with no distant shore. And worst of all, no Brother Smith. Not a clue of him. He'd always said it would someday happen, and it had. The lake was his Jordan.

Old Okeechobee had taken him home.

CHAPTER 4

I stumble ashore.

The pole light was the only light nearby.

There it stood, by itself, sticking up on the end of a shallow water ramp about three times the height of a man. Behind the short pier there was a two-building shanty, slanted roof, no lights inside. Blinking, I read a sign:

SATTERFIELD FISH CAMP
BOAT RENTALS . . . HOMEMADE PECAN PIE
SARAH SATTERFIELD, PROPRIETOR

I saw boats.

There were several of them, close to a dozen, but no oars. The boat nearest to me looked to be in a sorry shape. It was beached with a busted seat. And stove in.

My cut foot was smarting.

So I sat myself on an overturned boat, and hoisted my foot to my knee for a look. I had a bleeding gash about a finger long, or longer, and oozing blood.

I sighed.

As I faced the lake, looking across it, the distant waterline seemed to be getting lighter. This meant, according to Miss Hoe, that I was facing east, because that was where morning sun started to shine.

Somewhere, over there, was Brother Smith. What should I do now?

Reaching a hand inside my soaking wet shirt, I felt for my letter. It was safe. But gone was my two books; one had been Brother Smith's Bible that he'd give me, the other'd been a present from Miss Hoe. It was called *Tom Sawyer*.

I felt pain.

My foot sure was bleeding.

"Boy!"

A voice spoke, behind me.

Turning around, I spotted a couple of men, along with three dogs. Hounds. Short hair and long ears and leaner than dry-spell beans. Rib-counting lean. One of the dogs stared at me and bared his teeth. The dog growled. The taller of the two men wore a pistol that hung from a gunbelt. I couldn't see the entire gun, only the curve of its handle.

"Hey," the man said to me, coming my way. "Boy, how come you ain't with the rest? You aiming to run off?"

The shorter man said, "Yup, that's the way their kind usual behaves. Nothing fancy enough for them picker people. Except a good kick where it'll spur 'em toward a day's labor or along a row of produce."

I couldn't talk.

All I recalled of Shack Row, and Papa, sudden come rushing up into my throat, so's I could barely breathe.

The tall man pointed a finger at my neck.

"Where's your tag?"

"My what?" I asked him.

"Don't fake a fooly at me," the man said. "You

know, dang it all, what I just meant." He spat out a brown squirt of tobacco juice. "What's your number, boy? The number on your worker tag?"

"Ain't got one. I'm not . . ."

"What you fixing to pull, sonny boy? You best not try to make no jackass out of me. That what you're trying to do?"

"No. No, sir."

Because I couldn't seem to force myself to match a stare with either of these here gentlemen, I sort of hung my head, and looked down at their feet. That's when I took notice of what near to stopped my heart.

Both men were wearing *shoes.*

It frighted me to see such, because men with shoes had boss power. The short man bended over as though he was preparing to let one of the dogs loose . . . the one that'd snarled my way.

"Boy," the shorter guy said, "do you got any idea what just one of these here mutts can perform on you?"

"No . . . I don't."

The tall man wearing the gun grinned at me, a smile with no warm to it, just teeth. He spoke.

"Herman, right here . . . is my dog man. He got a vial of coon juice in his pocket. All we gotta do, boy, is yank off your wet little bloomers and then hogtie you butter-up to one of them fallen cypress logs." He chuckled. "Our wolf dogs aint' tore a coon more'n two week. So, if'n we was to smear a gob of that juice on you, then you'd git yourself a lot lighter."

I'd heared about what the men were talking to me. Huff Cooter said that it was how the new young men git *initiated* at the Jailtown Lumberyard. It was called getting *dogged.*

Putting a hand into his pocket, the short man pulled out a little bottle, then he holded it up for me to study.

24

"Here 'tis," he telled me.

"Boy," said the tall man, "I'm going to ask you one more time." He paused. "What's your tag number?"

"I don't have one. Honest."

He didn't answer me. Instead, he just turned to the other man. "Herman, you pull the cork out a that fancy bottle."

Herman pulled.

I heared a little *pop*.

"Now," said the tall fellow, "show this lying little whelp what'll happen, when a worker don't confess the truth around here. Give that horny bluetick a quick whiff of that there coon perfume."

Herman didn't let the hound smell the open bottle. Only the cork. One sniff, and that dog was near to crazy, and I knowed why. The dog's spine went rigid. He jumped around like a mad dog and then dragged his belly on the ground like he'd took a awful itch, one he didn't know how to scratch.

It was a spell before the male hound could contain down to control. The other two dogs didn't appear to be much calmer. Only a bit.

"My name," said the taller man, "is Mr. Boss."

"That's right," said the dog man, "and Mr. Boss hain't never cotton to field folks that don't hustle, and pay a decent respect. Hear?"

"I hear. But I'm not—"

The tall man whipped out his pistol.

"You shush, boy. Shut your uppity little picker mouth when yo betters is learning you to act proper."

I wanted to turn and splash back into Okeechobee, and maybe git away from these mean people. Or drown. I couldn't seem to run. All I done was to stand pat, as the man called Mr. Boss come close to me, grabbed my hair, forced me down to my knees, and halfway ripped off my shirt.

"Hey, you got dirt inside your shirt pocket, boy. That be field dirt. You's a picker."

"He don't got a work tag," the short man said.

"No."

"Probable tore it loose, to pitch it."

"Yeah," said Mr. Boss. "Okay now, boy, what's your number, the one you got assigned when you arrive here in style, off'n the sweat bus?"

"I'm . . . Arly Poole . . . and . . ." I tried to tell about my father's grave dirt, inside my shirt pocket.

One of his hands ripped my hair, and the other poked the end of the pistol barrel up under my chin.

"You . . . ain't . . . nobody. Here, no worker's got a name. Or a soul. You understand?" He jabbed my throat with the gun muzzle. "All you got, young'n, is a number. You'd had one. Yeah, and you'd tore it off from around your neck. So your next number won't be no tag."

He paused to suck in a breath.

"You'll git *burnt*."

CHAPTER 5

They did it.

At first, I didn't think that anybody would heat a branding iron in a fire, and then, again and again and again, press a lot of dots to somebody's chest.

The dots formed my number.

I didn't even know what number I was. I screamed. All I could do was not go crazy because it hurted so dreadful, and the stink of my cooking flesh made me want to puke. The best I could produce was dry heaves, as there weren't no food in me. And no water.

Afterward, they poured salty vinegar on me (this I could easy smell) so that my raw scars would scab quickly, and heal, and so I'd not have a infection and not be able to work. After I got branded, they put me on a mule wagon and it went somewhere to a shack made out of cement blocks that smelled like somebody had died there.

Nobody else was inside it.

There wasn't nothing at all on the floor. Only dirt, like Shack Row. No table. No chair or bench. Only a hole that smelled of where a lot of sick people had let it loose, from one end or the other.

One doorway, open, without a door.

And no windows.

Inside, where I lay on a pile of rags and broken glass, there weren't no air, very little light. Only the flies. I'd passed out after they'd dumped me inside; after coming to, the first thing I was aware of was a fly walking along my lips. It made me spit.

My body started to itch.

I scratched myself. The rags I was lying on was, no doubt, crawling with lice. The gnawing kind.

Sometimes I would sleep. Then, as my body jerked awake, I'd know where I was; or, to be more correct, I'd not know at all.

Jailtown had a name.

And so did our section, Shack Row.

Here, it wasn't real. It was as though I be living in No Place, and I sudden had become Nobody. In my remembering, once I'd been Arly Poole, son of Mr. Dan Poole, a produce picker. Mrs. Addie Cooter had lived next door, along with her five young. Huff Cooter was my best pal, my only. And his sister, Essie May Cooter, was the only girl I could ever dream about, hoping that someday she'd become my sweetheart.

It was daytime. And rainy.

I slept, and then it was evening, dusky out, and the trucks and wagons come, letting off pickers. Some of them had bottles of wine, and they entered the cement-block hut where I was lying on the buggy rags, looked at me, and then said nothing.

They was all ages. Some younger than I was.

All males.

One face after another bent down to look at me, into my eyes, without talking.

They didn't know that I was Arly Poole, and didn't want to know. It sudden come to me why. They be *numbers*. On a old man's chest, I could notice a brand, like mine, a bunch of dots that somehow spelled a work number. Some of the men wore tags around their necks.

"Who he be?" I heard someone ask.

"He new."

"Hey, poke in his clothes. See if he got any anything. And take it. We split."

Hands touched me.

None of the hands was too gentle. Finding nothing, somebody's foot presented me with a kick; it didn't hurt that much, because end-of-day pickers don't got a lot of strong for kicking.

I could smell my daddy.

He'd come home, on the sundown wagon, with Addie Cooter holding the ribbons to guide four mules. Dan Poole come wobbling home to Shack Row, at evening, his white body burnt from all day picking in a endless no-shade vegetable field. Somebody swore that a row of tomato plants stretched for a hundred miles. Miss Hoe, when I asked her, said that it was true.

One single tomato row actual go a hundred miles long. And there was rows by the hundreds.

A lot of Shack Rows too.

And all pickers.

Like us.

Lying there, wanting food and water, yet lacking the gumption to move or speak, I waited to die. Here, in No Place, there didn't seem to be any purpose in staying myself alive.

My chest burned like I was cooked meat.

After a spell, and along toward dark, an old white man come close to me and leaned down. His breath was wine rotten.

"Hey," he said. "I be Coo Coo."

I didn't answer.

"Mr. Boss's men tell me I ain't nobody no more."

He winked. "But I know different." The old man whispered low. "I got a *name*. Nobody here know I keept it."

"I got a name too. I'm Arly."

"Where's your tag?"

I pointed to my swollen chest.

Coo Coo looked, and turned away like it hurt him enough to puke. Then turned back to speak. "Me . . . I don't never understand them burnt numbers. Only that there Mr. Boss do, and he's hateful."

"Where am I?" I asked.

The old fellow shook his head, back and forth, and it seem he wouldn't be fixing to quit. "Don't nobody know. All I know is that we all at . . . at a *unload*."

"What?"

Coo Coo pointed at the open doorway.

"Bus come. We load on. Bus go, and it'll go some-time all night. Aboard the bus, we git a half a breadloaf, and a bottle of wine. Bus come to a stop. We all gotta git off and go pick. Nobody see or know nothing. All I see is when the blue bus come, I git on it and try to sleep . . . until the bus man cuts the motor . . . at the next unload."

Moving away from me, Coo Coo walked slow to the open bad-smelling ground hole, stood there with his legs apart, fumbled, and let loose his water. All the time he was doing it, I could hear a weak trickle of urine, and groans from Coo Coo like it was paining him fearful to empty his insides.

"Bad wine," Coo Coo said, returning to stand over me. "It's that sour wine that'll sting ya both ways, coming and going."

He sank to his knees.

I could smell cukes. It was a smell I'd knowed back in Jailtown, inside our shack, whenever Papa would come home from picking cucumbers. The cuke smell made me feel like Coo Coo was sort of like another Dan Poole. Not really. My daddy weren't crazy in the head.

Coo Coo weren't too regular.

It got dark.

A bus come. It was a dull blue with only three fenders. The left front fender be missing. It honked a horn three times, and then three more, and I could hear the engine cough to a quit. People voices all sounded a grumble and some swore.

"Load," I heard a strong voice say. "Y'all move it and right sudden now. Load on!"

Coo Coo's eyes widened. "We gotta *go*," he said. "We gotta load up the bus. If'n us pickers don't git on pronto, we don't git no pay . . . all what we git is a punish." He forced hisself to stand. "I can't take no punishing again. It hurts so bad I cry for days and nights . . . and can't sleep."

As Coo Coo pulled me to my feet, my chest seemed to be on fire. It hurt so that I was praying I'd pass out, or pass away.

"Where we going?"

"Hush, boy." He led me toward the doorway. "We ain't allowed to ask. No . . . no question. Ye git a punishment. So bad it'll twist your brain to nothing but a knot. The hurt'll pickle your thinking."

Outside there was a bus. A whole line of buses. Maybe five or six, painted different shades of blue. They looked like big hungry monsters that ate up pickers, one by one.

"Load. Load up."

Somebody pushed me and I fell. Then my rump got kicked by a pointed-toe boot, and the hurting of it turned my stomach sick.

We loaded on the blue bus that was missing a fender.

I sat beside Coo Coo.

A couple of men started to fight over a bus seat, but then stopped. Both appear to be too wore out to throw a punch. Or even spit.

"Coo Coo, where they taking us?"

"You don't ask. Nobody know."

"Are we prisoners?"

"We ain't even so much as that."

CHAPTER 6

The bus window was cracked.

Also, the glass was stained a sick yellowy color, but I looked to my left and saw a fading sunset, so pretty and soft, and sadly dying.

It told me that the bus was moving north.

Night come complete.

With every mile the bus chugged, the weather turned cold. Colder than I'd ever recalled. All I had on was my damp shirt and pants. Nobody around had much more. Next to me, I could feel old Coo Coo shaking as he slept. Florida people never wear nothing more'n a shirt.

It got colder.

Inside me, there weren't no food. Seems I'd ate a day or so ago, but couldn't recall exact when. Across the bus's walkway a man was actual sobbing. Inch by inch, we all sort of moved away from the windows, to crowd together.

I couldn't stop myself shaking.

Coo Coo was doing the same, his skinny old white body almost rattling as loud as the bus engine. If he'd had teeth, they'd be chattery as mine. It helped to hold my breath, and strain; then let it out, and suck in air again. It was also a help, but not much, to press my hands against the upright back of the seat in front of me, and push.

I pushed real hard.

For a long time.

"Oh, Lordy me," said Coo Coo, half asleep. "We gotta git off'n this cussed bus machine and crank up a fire. I'm afeared I'm next to die."

We was all herded now, close to as many others as we could possible git.

The stink of those people was enough to make me want to quit breathing. I kept my mouth open, so's I wouldn't snort in their awful smell up my nose. It didn't help.

Closing my eyes, and hanging on to Coo Coo, I started wondering if maybe I'd already died. Maybe I actual did drown in Lake Okeechobee, like the way Brother Smith went down. People sometimes would say that "a man died and was now cold in his grave." So I guessed that's what dying was like.

Death was cold.

Coo Coo shook worse and worse.

I figured that any minute this old-timer was due to leave go of life, and I'd lose the only person I knowed by name.

"Oh," he groaned, "oh, I'm fixing to freeze."

He kept mumbling. His words didn't make a whole bunch of sense. Just a clump of noises that sometimes sounded close to talking. He spoke about somebody he must've knowed, a person whose name was Hattie.

"Oh, Hattie . . . I'm so cold. Old and cold and broke down drunk. I can't even shoot a stick of pool no more. Or play cards. Ain't never git no aces. Got no kings . . . no queens. Can't hit a sider, not in no side pocket, man. Can't allow to sink a ball, solid or stripe.

Stripers is good to eat. Oh, I be hungry, Hattie. If I fetch wood, you'll fry up some frits. Some of your best hot muffins."

He went on and on.

All night, as it became even colder, I hung close to Coo Coo as I could git. His breathing sounded like Papa's. Cloudy, and full of sick stuff. Sorry lungs.

But, at least while this old picker was breathing, it meant Coo Coo was still alive.

If I could hear him, so was I.

"Hattie . . . Hattie . . ."

Sometimes, during the night I'd say "Brother Smith" or "Miss Hoe . . . Miss Binnie Hoe and Mrs. Newell." I tried thinking about how much I wanted to kiss Essie May Cooter, and hug Essie close to me.

"Hattie . . . you're my . . ."

The bus stopped.

I heared the driver cut the engine. After that, he opened the only bus door, and went outside. Soon he come back and yelled at us. Only one word:

"Unload."

Nobody moved, or seemed to want to.

"Hattie . . ."

"*Unload*, ya stinking stoopers!"

Through the bus window, I could see no town, no shacks. Not a board in sight. Nothing except bushes and brambles. As somebody in front of me moved a mite, I could see the bus driver actual drag people to their feet, and then pushing 'em out the door. He was darn near to throwing 'em out into the night. The words he was using weren't too friendly.

"Where we at?" somebody ask. "I ain't going outside in the cold darkness and pick no nothing."

Men were yelling, screaming, and begging not to

git tossed off the bus. The driver was blowing a whistle. He blowed it really loud.

"Unload."

All the buses stopped in a line to empty their complaining cargo. Nearby, a man was passing around a jug. He wasn't asking anyone if he wanted a drink. He was ordering each and every worker to swallow some.

Another man was yanking loaves of bread in two, tossing half a loaf to every person. "Eat," he said. "It'll help fight the weather. We can't earn no money off you pickies if y'all freeze up and die. So *eat*. Hear?"

I ate. So did Coo Coo.

Because the bread was so stale, it felt like little hunks of busted concrete inside my mouth. I had to force it down my gullet. Coo Coo took a pull on the liquor jug, coughed, spat up, and then helped hisself to another gulp. The second made him cough even worse.

"Nobody'll want to put a mouth to that jug after old Coo Coo," a man said. "Not me."

He was wrong.

The pickers all drank like they didn't much care if'n they lived or passed. Even I tried to swallow some. But it was mean tasting. I'd have traded a whole jug of it for a sip of hot tea.

Everybody milled around in a tight circle.

Nobody wanted to be left on the outside, not in that cold wind. Years back, Papa and I had survived a few frosty nights in Shack Row, nights when we stayed awake to shove more wood sticks into our little cookstove.

"This night," a picker said, "won't never end up."

The bus driver told us that nobody would be allowed to get back inside the bus unless he first piddled his water. I tried, strained, but nothing emptied out of me. Not a drop.

Even if'n I'd been bloated to go, I couldn't have, because I was so cold, all over.

"*Load.*"

The driver pushed people to the bus.

"Load up."

One man darted away, into the shadows of the night. A gun was fired, once, then twice. Right after the third shot, I heard a voice yelp, a ways off. Then I saw a dog man dragging the wounded fellow back to a bus, not ours.

The dog's back was arched, like he'd got bred to bait pickers who'd try to escape.

The men kicked the bleeding man.

"Easy," somebody warned them, "because if you kick his skull in, he don't work in the morning. Ya can't charge a grover if we deliver a corpse." He chuckled. "All these dirties got to be is barely breathing."

"Reckon you're right on that, Broward."

"Okay, let's *load.*"

"*Load!*"

I didn't want to put myself back on that blue bus. Yet I was too fearful to stay away out here in a night of nothing. Maybe, in luck, this bus could stop at Moore Haven, or even Jailtown.

But that didn't make sense.

We'd come a long way. Many hours, close to a full night long, or so I guessed. We'd just not be too nearby to anyplace I'd know. Maybe not even old Okeechobee.

Mounting the bus, I sighed.

About now, I'd settle for Mr. Roscoe Broda and Shack Row and Jailtown, all to one. At least I'd be home. Dinker Witt and his wife would take care of me, and feed me a meal. But here, I was lost.

"I'm to die," I said to Coo Coo as the two of us sat in the two-seater, close as possible to some others. "Soon I'll be dead, Coo Coo."

"Maybe," he said, "we already are."

I wondered if this blue bus was Hell.

CHAPTER 7

Morning come.

The buses stopped, and the drivers all started blowing their whistles. The sound scratched my ears. "Unload. Unload."

Coo Coo didn't move.

I poked him.

"Coo Coo," I said to him. "Be you alive?"

"Hattie . . ."

"No. I'm Arly. My name's Arly Poole."

His eyes opened. "Where we at?" he asked.

Looking out of the cracked window, I saw several sheds of gray boards. The ground was covered with pine needles and cones, plus a couple of dozen empty wine bottles.

Somebody, I could smell, was cooking.

"Unload!" The bus driver was unpiling our heap of near-to-frozen bodies, yanking a arm here and a leg there. Still blowing his sharp whistle. "Y'all unload. Hear? Now."

Getting up first, I helped Coo Coo to stand. He rubbed the gray stubble on his face. His hands were still soiled dirty from yesterday's field work, his fingers stained a dark green from the cuke vines. Coo Coo's hands appeared to me like they couldn't never begin to wash up clean, not even if he'd scrub all day.

"Unload. There's chow."

The driver's promise of food didn't seem to hustle any of the pickers. They moved as I'd knowed all field hand to move, and that was at turtle speed. Stiffer than stone.

"Food. Food! Everybody out now."

We stumbled out of the blue bus.

Even though the sun was just up, the air was chilly, and windy. Some of the weeds by the roadside had droopy leaves, curling into their own private death. Frost burnt. The green was weakening to gray.

"Where's the food, Coo Coo?"

"Who cares." The old fellow scratched his crotch. "I'd rather have me one burny drink of liquor. Cold booze is better than hot oatmeal. Least it ain't lumpy."

He almost made me laugh.

I spotted the chow line, such as it was. More like a chow fight, on account some of the stronger men were fisting to be first.

"Come on," I said, pulling Coo Coo along with me. "We best eat, whatever it turns out to be, or the cold'll beat us down."

"Oh, all right," he said. "Whether we eat or no, we still gotta pay for it. And pay high."

The two of us waited patient until we was the last to a feeding. Their food weren't worth a fight over.

Breakfast was bread and soup. The bread was cold, and stale, but the whatever-it-was soup was hot. Mostly hot water, a few grains of cooked barley, beans, corn, some limpy collards. It smelled a bit fishy.

"It's good," I told Coo Coo.

It wasn't. Not at all. But I had to urge Coo Coo to eat it. He'd purpose let me use his shoulder as a pillow.

All we had was a bowl to each man. No spoons. We lifted the bowls and gulped. Some of Coo Coo's spilled on his ratty old shirt, yet he didn't seem to notice it none. No bother.

I wanted to keep Coo Coo alive. First, I sort of liked him, because he was the only person who talked at me, back at the other place, in the cement box. Second, he might not be as nutty as he let on, and perhaps knowed the names of places, some of which could pan out to be neighborly to Moore Haven. Third, it wouldn't harm me to lend a hand to help another person. After all, Miss Hoe and Mrs. Newell and Brother certain assisted me.

Brother Smith died for me.

Coo Coo caught a fish bone in his throat, from the chowder, and I helped him stand while he was coughing it out. His eyes were all watery red, but smiling.

"Thanks," he said.

Nobody else even bother to notice. There and then, Coo Coo could've passed out dead and no other picker would even bat an eye. Not for a crazy old coot. Perhaps not for anyone.

When there's little to eat, poor food, and all the eaters are half starved, a meal before a workday doesn't take up much time. A minute or so later, the whistles was blowing again.

"Load! Load! Load!"

We loaded.

The buses pulled away from the gray sheds, and then turned down a red clay road. I smelled smoke. But even by looking around, I couldn't learn whatever was smoking. It certain didn't smell like eats.

To my nose, the smell was hard and black.

Almost mean.

The smoke become thicker on both sides of the clay

road. Beyond the smoke, the short trees seemed to be in rows. Row after row. Endless. Squinting through the dirty glass, I saw the fruit on every tree.

Oranges.

The buses was final stopped.

"Unload."

"I'll be," said Coo Coo, as we unloaded from the blue bus. "It's a orange grove." He smiled. "I ain't et me a decent orange in more'n a year. Been doing vegetables."

We lined up.

Most of the men reported their work tag numbers when asked. Coo Coo done it so. But I didn't know mine.

A guy in big boots come along to peek inside my shirt and read my chest burn. He marked it to a paper on a clipboard. Maybe this meant that I was to earn money. Well, I didn't even have a penny, so maybe I'd eventual arrive to Moore Haven and not make my entrance busted broke.

Coo Coo got told to pick oranges.

I didn't.

Instead, it was my job to service the smudge pots, to keep a whole row fueled and burning. It was smoky work. Made me cough and my eyes run.

Coo Coo appeared.

"Here," he said, tossing me a orange. "Eat up."

"Am I allowed?"

Coo Coo spat. "Any dude that labors where there's eats growing, and goes hungry, ain't nobody except a Simple Simon."

I ate it.

No oranges growed in Jailtown. Long ago, I'd ate a orange, but it was so far back in the past I couldn't clear remember the flavor. After the first bite, I knew. A cold orange tasted like it looked. Real pretty. When nobody was looking, I ate another. And more. My teeth hurt, so I had to eat really slow and careful, a small bite at a time.

The oranges weren't froze.

Close to it. Sort of like eating winter.

Working near the smudge pots final got me warm enough to believe that I was maybe almost half alive, and intending to stay so.

Coo Coo returned.

He ran a lot like a lame turkey, gimpy legged, with his meatless shoulders hunching on a slant, the left higher than the right. The way he moved, I could easy tell that Coo Coo was toting something inside the front of his shirt.

"Here," he said, out of breath. He handed the warm things over to me. "I found this on the ground back yonder. Somebody dropped it, so's I snatched it up real quicksome, for us two to split. Half and half."

It was a entire chain of sausages, linked together. Ten in all. Coo Coo ate five and so did I. They was warm and fresh cooked. Real tasty, after we'd wiped off the grit. Mouth full, Coo Coo snorted a grin, then chewed careful and swallowed his fifth and last.

"It's *boss* food. Cooked special for a field boss. Us pickies don't git to gobble eats as fancy as this."

"Thanks," I said. "You're good to share it."

"Aw, it ain't nothing. I figured you was toiling on empty. And I couldn't eat all of 'em. I'd have me nothing but some gas and a gut ache." Bending, he held his hands close to a smudge pot. "Wow," he said, "that feels comforty."

Looking at him, I sudden come to a realize that Coo Coo was the only friend I had right now. Maybe

I'd never git to Moore Haven. So, for today, it'd be Coo Coo and me . . . against the world.

"I like you, Coo Coo."

He smiled. "I like you too." He paused to wipe sausage grease off his mouth with a shirtsleeve. "Say, what did you tell me your name is? I forgit."

"Arly."

"How come you befriend a old geezer like me?"

"You smell like my father."

CHAPTER 8

Coo Coo picked all day.

"I can't wait until quitting time," he said. "My lame old backbone sure is screaming to ease myself down to leisure."

"Me too," I told him.

"My guess," said Coo Coo, "is that I'll have to maybe fill this here orange bag only a couple-three more times, and the whistle'll blow."

It never did blow for me. The crew boss decided that another cold night was coming due. More smudge pots arrived on a flatbed truck, got unloaded, and demanded all-night-long attention.

The pickers would sleep in the buses.

I wouldn't, I got told.

"Boy, you're to work through the night. Come morning, if you keep all them smudge fixed up, we'll see to it that you git a bonus. It's extra pay. Cash money. And that's exact what you'll be got coming to you, kiddo. What's your number?"

Opening my shirt, I showed him my chest.

The crew boss winced.

"Oh," he said, "I see you been a troublemaker. Best you don't cause enough mischief to Mr. Boss, or he might give you a punishment. A lashing. You ain't fixing to scoot off in the night, and give us men grief, are ya?"

"No, sir, I sure ain't."

"Good. You just keep all them smudge pots smoking. The heat and the black smoke is what'll save them oranges."

He left.

I was too tired to wonder how much money my bonus would be. Ought to be double a day's pay. I was ample smart enough to figure that out, even without Miss Hoe.

All night long, I toted the empty fuel buckets to the oil barrel, turned the crank, and then returned to feed oil to all my smudge pot tanks. Only three pots died out, but I manage to light 'em all up again.

In the night, I'd heard dogs and gunshots . . . like some picker had tried to scamper off.

Later, somebody screamed. It was a man's voice screaming high up, like a woman in pain. I didn't want the hurting person to be Coo Coo.

"God," I said, looking up through the smoke toward the stars, "please don't let 'em punish Coo Coo."

More time passed.

The night was staying dark. And all my smudge pots kept on roaring their fire.

Hearing a noise, like footsteps, I turned and spotted my friend. "Coo Coo," I said, "how come you're here?"

Arms wrapped around his own chest, Coo Coo advance toward the pot I was tending, to come close.

"Can't sleep," he said, coughing.

"Why not?"

"It's too dang blessed chilly in that blue bus. Some

of the windows is busted. So I come to look you up, and maybe beg a lick or two of smoke heat." He chuckled. "It's so freaky cold that even our bus turned blue."

His old body was shaking.

"Never again," he telled me. "No, not never even a one time am I gonna complain about the heat of sunshine when I'm next out picking. No. Never again. Not a one time." He give a shudder. "I don't guess I can recall balmy old Floridy even cooling down to this weather. We must be up north."

He inched closer to the pot.

"Caution," I said to Coo Coo, "or you'll possible scorch yourself a chest like mine."

"It still hurt?" He sounded like he cared.

I nodded. "Keeps me warm."

He shot me a snaggletooth grin. "Arly, you are a brave child. Yessir, a very brave one. Your daddy'd be right proudly of you. Indeedy so."

"And you're a cold man. Stay here by the heat, and maybe I can go swipe us each a blanket. Or a tarp."

Coo Coo held up a hand. "No. Don't go, Arly. If you git catched stealing, big tall Mr. Boss, or somebody, will crack down on you hard. Hang you maybe."

"Hang me?" My throat tightened.

Coo Coo pointed a crooked finger at me. "Them punishment boys won't actual kill you dead. Us tag workers is all the income they got. But what they'll do is hang you upside down, a rope around both your ankles. Then they suspend you from a tree limb . . . over a smudge pot. And all that black smoke'll suck straight up your lungs."

"Have you ever seen 'em do such?"

He nodded. "Oh, yes. Too many times. A upside-downer will beg to have those boys shoot him, smack a bullet into his heart or his head, to end the torture."

"How come you work for Mr. Boss?"

Coo Coo shook his head and shrugged. "I dunno. Got drunk, I guess. Come to, and there was a work tag around my neck, and a brass band of a headache between my ears. Besides, I was broke, so I had to earn a keep somehow."

"How long ago was that?"

"Long. Lots of years."

"You ought to run off, Coo Coo. You honest ought."

He stared at me. "Run off? Me? On my poorly old legs I don't guess I could outrun a three-legged snail, even if he's going uphill and me down."

I caught myself actual laughing. "Coo Coo, you certain do got a wit inside you. A regular funny bone, you be." I clapped my hand on his shoulder.

"Arly . . ."

"Yes."

"Are we pals?"

I smiled. "We sure are."

Coo Coo retreated a inch or so away from the smudger, like he was cooked meat, ready to carve.

"You final warm?" I asked, hoping so.

"Final be."

"Good."

He stood up. "Arly, I got to figure a way to git you away from this picker crew."

My heart leaped. But the thought of a *punishment* was a threaten on my mind, as the say-so goes. It was inside my brain, beating on me, like a big mean drum. I didn't really know exact what Mr. Boss and the other men would do to me. It was the fear of what I didn't know, and could only imagine, that spooked into my thinking.

The old fellow was quiet for a time. He just hunkered down to look at the yellowy fire in the smudge pot like it somehow had took a purchase on his soul and wouldn't leave go.

"Arly," he said, not looking up, "I got me a honest-to-goodness real special somebody. I ain't even seen him as yet. But I had a pitcher of him . . . until it got lost."

"A picture of who?"

Coo Coo smiled. "I got me a . . . a grandson."

"Where?"

"I forgit. My boy's child. Then I got stupid fall-down-and-shirttail drunk, lost the pitcher, and now I can't recall the little boy's name. Every time I admit that I disremember, the guilty of it chases me into liquor, and I drink the bottle vacant."

He squatted by the smudge pot, without a move or a twitch, while I took some empty oil containers to the barrel, cranked oil, and fed the pots that begged my tending.

Coo Coo was still there when I returned.

"I got an idea," I said. "Maybe, now just maybe, your son named his little boy after *you*. his name could be . . . Little Coo Coo. Or whatever." I paused to think. "Coo Coo isn't your real and righteous name, is it?"

I waited for him to answer me.

He final did.

"No."

"Well, what's your name? Mine is Arly Poole. Seems like, if we're fixing to be pals, I ought to know yourn." I grinned. "For sure, your old mama didn't born you and name you Coo Coo."

"No, I reckon not."

"Well, so what do you proper get called?"

Coo Coo looked up at me. "Nobody calls me a correct way no more. I ain't heared a soul use my Christian name, not in a whole sweet bunch of years."

"What is it? I'll use it if'n you cotton it."

Coo Coo smiled. "It's . . . Charles."

CHAPTER 9

It came to be morning. At last.

By first light, I was starting to doubt that I could fetch back one more can of fuel oil, or look to another pot.

Coo Coo was sleeping.

He was curled up snug beside the hottest smudge pot, his thin white hair resting on a little mound of pine needles that I'd swept in for his comfort. In a way, it was a bit like how I used to tend my father.

"Sweet dreams, Charles," I said.

As I studied him I sort of guessed that good old Coo Coo weren't nearly as nutty as he posed to be. Inside, as I saw him, he had control of his thinking and could still run his brain.

Charles, I figured, was no fool. Oh, for certain, he possible pretend to be one, in order to confuse Mr. Boss. Or to try likewise against the enforcer gang, men with tracker dogs, and belt pistols. And ropes.

But was Coo Coo foolish?

The more I listened to him, the smarter this old codger seemed to be. A drunk? Yes. Oh, yet nary a Simple Simon, as he'd earlier said.

The crew boss come around.

Lucky for little old Arly Poole, all my smudge pots happen to be smoking away like a giant's cigar. Think black smoke was billowing upward from every pot that was under my tending.

As for me, I was about near to fall over, place my face into mud, and sleep until the next comet.

"Boy."

I looked at the crew boss.

"You done a decent job here. What's your tag?"

I shook my head. "Sir, I don't got a tag. It was all a mistake. Honest. You know I can work."

The boss didn't say a word.

"My name is Arly Poole. I'm from Jailtown. I was on my way to Moore Haven, sir, and a sculler boat swamped out over Okeechobee, and Brother Smith put me across a oar. He drown. Went clean under like a lead sinker weight on a fishing line. Honest. I'm Arly Poole. And I got me a letter."

The man nodded, as if he was deaf. Then, shifting his attention, he looked down at Coo Coo, who was still out, still asleep, right close to a smudger.

"He your granddaddy?"

I was fixing to say "no." But something made me stop and study it all. It could be possible that the crew boss wouldn't want to split a grandfather and a grand-child.

"Grandpa, wake up," I then said.

"He drunk again?"

"No," I said, kneeling next to Coo Coo. "He's only tuckered out. Mister, you ought to see my grand-daddy pick oranges. He picked more'n any pair of pickers in the entire grove. He ought to git extra food."

"You two look out for each other, do you? Sort of keep each other healthy and ready to do work?"

"Yes," I fibbed. "That's how we actual do."

"Good. You doing okay. You'll git a bonus this week."

"A cash bonus?"

The man's eyes narrowed. "Now, don't you question me, picker boy. True, we give a bonus in cash money if'n it suits our purpose, at the time. If it don't, why then you and your old granddaddy'll git a store credit. And that's every dang bit as legal as cash."

For a minute, I remember. I recalled every Saturday night at Jailtown. All us pickers from Shack Row would line up in town, at Mrs. Stout's store, to collect our wages for six days under a Florida sun, harvesting produce.

But there was always a shack rent, or half wages, or some sort of a fine for doing this or that . . . and it somehow come to what Mrs. Stout called a negative tally. That meant that us Pooles stilled *owed*, instead of collecting.

We never seemed to crawl out from under.

Always the same.

A debt.

"Where's the store?" I asked.

The man briefly looked away. "Well, boy, it happens to be in Miami. That's our company headquarters. Got us a store over here, real fancy, and all you pickies can stop in, any time, and take advantage of the total store credit that our bonus affords you. Fair and square."

Staring at him, I was wondering how a growed-up man could tell a kid about some faraway store credit. The so-call store probable weren't there at all.

"Fair and square," I said, knowing that I'd hustle around all night, for nothing except a empty promise . . . credit at a store I'd never live to visit.

The weather final turned warmer, which meant they let the smudge pots go cold.

I slept in the bus.

The pickers kept on snipping oranges off the orange trees until there weren't a single orange hanging.

"Load!"

It woke me up again.

Coo Coo returned, and our blue bus (which somebody said used to be a school bus) fired up its engine, and left the orange grove.

None of us got paid.

Not a one.

Around the middle of the day, our fleet of buses stopped somewhere (I didn't know where, and neither did Coo Coo), and we got ordered to unload. Again bread, and wine bottles. No soup. We be cooked no breakfast. The night before I'd not eaten a bite of supper, so I wolfed in the bread as if a thief was there to steal it off my hand.

Between gulps on his wine bottle, Coo Coo said, "You didn't take no wine."

"No, I don't like it."

He grunted. "Like it or not, you'll git charge for it. They'll ledger it against your tag. Your number."

"They do that?"

Coo Coo nodded.

"Yeah, and what they'll dock every picker is twice what the wine's worth. Or maybe more." He burped. "I oughta know, on account I been a wino for most my life."

"Load! Load. Load up."

Our buses all filled and moved on.

Miles later, after I been asleep and awake and asleep again, we stopped and unloaded somewhere. Spot after spot. Yet none of these places ever seemed to have itself a name. For pickers, places was a lot like people.

No names.

"Where we at, Coo Coo?" I kept asking.

He'd shrug and say, "Beats me."

The places were different ones, but they were sort of all alike. Hard work, no bed to sleep on (only the bus), cruddy food, and a bottle of wine. Or, when there weren't no wine, somebody'd come around with a bucket of warm dirty water with a dipper in it.

If one man caught sick, we all did.

I figured it was the dipper.

It never got washed even a one time, and I'd wager that the bucket received equal care.

All us pickers got the runs. Coo Coo called it the Back Door Trots. My bowels went loose a dozen times a day, even when I was sleeping on the blue bus. Any time there was a hand water pump, or a hose hooked up to a shed, I'd squirt myself clean, and do the same for my shirt and trousers.

Both were wearing to raggy.

Coo Coo looked worse. When he wasn't asleep, he was drunk, and mumbling in his half-crazy way about a Hattie somebody. I never ask who Hattie be and Coo Coo didn't tell me.

Days went by.

And weeks.

I'd forgot, after a stretch, who I was and that my name was Arly Poole.

One evening, Coo Coo happened to be sober; either that, or too sick to drink his wine. It was a strange sort of evening, but I couldn't decide why. Coo Coo give me a present. A small used shirt he'd found. He'd tried to wash it, so it didn't smell too bad of somebody else's sweat.

I thanked Coo Coo and then asked him, "How come you done this for me?"

He told me. "It's Christmas."

CHAPTER 10

Winter was over.

All us pickers got a day off.

No work. It was Sunday. And then Coo Coo woke me up to say he had news. "Christers are coming."

"Who?"

"Oh, some Holy Joe and his troop of singing sisters. Bible thumpers."

"Do we gotta go?"

Coo Coo shook his head. "No, we don't *got* to. But maybe it'll benefit us both to attend. You never know what the religious folks will dish out."

"Food?"

"Maybe."

"We could use some clothes."

Coo Coo looked down at his pantlegs where his dirty knees were poking through into the weather. "Reckon we could."

"Do I have to wash?" I asked the Coo Coo as we stepped off the bus.

"Naw," he said. "Don't give it a bother. Sometimes, if these Sky Hawkers see ya tore and dirty, they break out their better loot."

"How come they're here today?"

Coo Coo snorted. "To fish."

Ahead of us, a few pickies had already arrived. People were singing a song . . . about God. It was so easy to tell, even from a distance, which was which in the group.

First off, our bunch was quiet. Pickers were sort of part naked. Gaps in everything they had on. "A picker's shirt," Coo Coo had said more'n once, "is a stink with holes in it."

Holy Joe and his followers were all dressed in black. The leader had a black hat, a black string tie, a long black hammerclaw coat, black pants. The ladies were in black bonnets and dresses to match.

What was so surprising was that every single one of them Christers wore *shoes.*

Black shoes.

After the song, the Holy people fetched out some shiny brass gadgets and blew into them and assembled one heck of a racket. They even pounded on a big drum, a little drum, and a jingling tambourine. The people blowed really hard until their faces sweated, and their cheeks blushed red.

Their musical piece final managed to blow itself out like a blast of bean gas.

The Holy Joe stood on a box.

"Brothers and Sisters," he began, holding a big book. It was, to nobody's surprise, black. "If you please, allow me to introduce myself to you, my congregated friends."

He smiled a warm smile.

Looking at Holy Joe, I saw a man who was maybe fifty years old, short and stout, and very clean pink hands. Even his fingernails. His black shoes were shinier than a darky's ass.

"My name," he telled us, "is John Patrick Mulligan.

I'm called *Our Father* J. P. Mulligan, and I am a duly sworn Golden Prophet of Salvation. We, in our blessed church, one that I am proud to confess that I personally founded, have come to *save* you. Because, today is not just another ordinary Sunday. No, today is . . . Easter Sunday."

Yanking a hanky rag from his pants pocket, Our Father Mulligan wiped his ruddy face. His hanky weren't black! It was whiter than virtue.

"Now, then," the man said, "perchance you good parishioners are wondering just how I happened to have my title: Our Father. I shall explain. It is an honorary bestowal, and my title was bestowed upon me . . ."

Leaning down to my ear, Coo Coo whispered, "Yeah, it was bestowed upon me by *me*. He thunk it up my hisself."

I let that one sink in.

"We are here assembled," the man in black said, "so that I may preach at you . . . I meant to say preach *for* you . . . on the fatal subject"— he pointed directly at Coo Coo—"of *SIN*."

Coo Coo flinched.

Yet he didn't bolt. He held ground.

"Sin," repeated Our Father, "sneaks up upon us in many vile and contemptuous disguises. Many false faces."

"Coo Coo," I whispered low, "when is Holy Joe fixing to pass out stuff? I'm so hungry that my stomach is emptier than that big old drum that they hit with a potato masher."

"Later," he answered. "They always torture you first."

"*Sin*," shouted Our Father John, jabbing a chubby finger at the sky, "is indeed the foul enemy of us all. You and I are brethren. We both toil and sweat in the

vineyards of righteousness, for the glory of Jehovah."
He glanced at the ladies.

"Amen," mumbled the black-dressed Sisters, sounding like it was their duty to chime in, on command.

The Holy Joe looked pleased, for a breath, and nodded a brief approval at the ladies and their response.

"Is that the end?" I asked Coo Coo as we stood side by side under a oak tree. "Do you think he'll pass out eats right now?"

"Nope."

"He won't?"

"No, he'll keep on abusing our ears until *we pass out.*"

Coo was right.

Our Father kept right on.

Sin seemed to be his favorite subject, and as far as I could understand, the Holy Joe was against it. He said that all of us were sinners. Yet we were lucky blessed with souls, even the lowest among us. As he said so, he looked right at *me.*

"Fire!" shouted Holy Joe.

Looking around, I couldn't spot any flames or smoke, and so I turned back to the sermon.

"Fire," repeated Our Father, "is what is eternally burning down in Hell . . . and that is your destination on the Road of Sin. The scorching inferno to consume a wayward soul. But," he paused to gasp, "there is another road. The upward stairs. Our church . . . the Golden Prophets of Salvation."

Again he pointed at Coo Coo.

"Brother," he asked him, "have you been *saved?*"

Coo Coo smiled and nodded at Father.

"Twenty-three times," he said.

Holding his Bible high in the air, he fired another

blast at Coo Coo. "Do not blaspheme," he warned. "Your spirit is in peril, Brother. Your heart is empty."

"Not near as empty," Coo Coo whispered to me, "as my paunch or my pocketbook."

"Empty as me," I said.

"It says clearly in the Holy Bible," ranted the Holy Joe, "that it is more blessed to *give* than to receive. The Road to Heaven is for the giving, the givers, those who freely and unselfishly *give*."

"Amen," droned the Sisters.

One of the Sisters was sort of young. My size. She winked at me, and I thought that she slightly looked like Essie May Cooter, only a little more to the plump side.

My stomach growled.

"Golly," I muttered to Coo Coo, whose belly had hardly been church-mouse quiet, "is that Our Father gent going to pass out stuff, or not?"

"Hold patient, Arly. He'll git to the key important part right quicksome, as you'll soon discover."

I did soon discover it.

Coo Coo had been correct. The Holy Joe so widely acclaimed as Our Father final did get around to pass something out. And, when it happened, it certain come as a surprise to me, to Coo Coo, and all the rest of the congregation.

For the rest of my days on earth, I'd never forget Our Father John Patrick Mulligan and his sisters. I'd always remember that religious group as the Golden Profits.

Yes, they passed something out that Easter.

They passed Our Father's hat.

CHAPTER 11

Days passed.
The rains come.

Florida heated up hotter than a griddle. Even in shade. But a picker doesn't have any shade at work. Nary a stick of it. For years I rubbed lard on my daddy's burnt back, because Dan Poole had never worked in shade during the all of his life.

Only beneath a cooker of a sun.

When you're stooped, as Coo Coo and I were day after day, there wasn't no shade along the endless rows of every kind of vegetable anybody could name.

Melons, cucumbers, limas, sweet potatoes, greens, celery, tomatoes, peas, beans, lettuce, cabbage, carrots . . .

It made me wonder how the growers could ever find enough people to eat it all. Bag upon bag. Baskets full. Truckloads, and then trainloads. I picked each vegetable one at a time, working so long in the soil that I'd become nothing but a vegetable myself.

Between two rows of produce there runs a little narrow dirt road. A roadway for us pickers. Little wide. But so long that you can't begin to see where the lane started, or where it might end. For me, it was the road of life.

Also a road of death. Almost every day or so, a picker would die on his long narrow alley of shadeless death.

I waited for it to happen to Coo Coo.

The summer heat was frying him into a skinny strip of red leather inside a rag. He was bending over yellow squash, on his knees, panting like a whipped dog. Each breath laboring as hard as he did on the produce. Whenever he'd slow down, I'd make certain to toss a squash into his bag instead of my own.

Coo Coo would look at me like he really was my granddaddy, but couldn't spit out a "thank you" through his dry, cracked lips.

He didn't have to. Not for me.

Afternoons it would usual rain. Not always. Rainless days were the killers.

But when the rain final come, so thick you couldn't recognize the worker on the other side of the vegetable row, the cooling water was a blessing. We never quit our picking, rain, or no rain. I'd stand up in the rainfall, letting its shower wash me clean and cool. For a hour or so afterward, the air weren't dusty at all, and was actual fit to haul into a lung.

Under the rain, all us pickers stood up tall.

It was like a prayer. Every face uplifted, looking at the storming sky, and giving a silent thanks. Each man in his own way.

Our baptism.

Oh, the raindrops did sting. It felt like being bited by a hundred chiggers at one time. Again and again. But the little pinchers of pain didn't real matter. It was a good hurt that didn't last. A herd of tiny needles nipping you alive.

"I'm not dead," I'd say. "I am Arly Poole."

Funny, but I could only say such during a heavy rain. And only to the sky. I'd thank God for my letter.

I didn't know any prayers.

Brother Smith had told Huff Cooter and me, a time ago, that it weren't necessary to put words to a prayer. Because a prayer wasn't said, it was felt. A silent secret that a person whispered to the Lord.

Sometimes I had the urge to shout it loud, fearing that God Himself wouldn't listen to a orphan.

I loved rain.

Because it was a gift from Heaven, only for picker people, like Coo Coo and me. And my father. Rain didn't bless the bosses. At the first timid drop, a crew boss ran for cover, under a shelter. It usual pleased me to watch a boss man scurry for a truck, git below a wagon, or duck into a shed. The bosses wouldn't receive the blessing. Dry folks were never bathed by the Lord.

Sometimes, during a rain, the thunder would warn us ahead of time. Then the lightning would crack the sky into broken pieces. Like a busted purple roof.

"Lie down, Arly."

Coo Coo usual forced me flat, sometimes even in a puddle of wet muck. He'd not allow me to stand up below lightning.

"You'll be toast," he'd warn.

Never did I quite understand the heat of lightning until one afternoon, during a cracker-boomer of a electric storm, when I actual saw the lightning hit a tree. There was the rain, pelting hard. That big old pine must've been drenchy wet, but it burnt like a torch. All aflame.

Coo Coo and I both watched.

Standing there in the rain, he nudged me. "Now you seen it happen," he said. "And if lightning can do such to a big old pine, think what it'll perform on a child . . . or even a growed man."

From then on, at about the first nearby bolt, I'd flatten myself like a lily pad, or close to, and remain flat until the storm passed us by.

"You're learning," Coo Coo said.

It was 1928.

Years have numbers, just like us field hands. I'd learnt that last year when Miss Hoe, our first and only schoolteacher, come to Jailtown. And a year is chopped into twelve parts, called months, and this month was August.

At night some of the people talked about a orphan man named Mr. Hoover who was going to be our next president. He wasn't yet. The president's today name I already knowed:

Mr. Calvin Coolidge of Vermont.

I'd asked Coo Coo where Vermont was located and what it was like in there, but Coo Coo claimed he honest didn't know, because the only place he'd knowed was right here . . . in Florida.

That was the day when Coo Coo happened to squint out of our blue bus window and then near to jumped up out of his seat.

"Boy," he said, " I know where we be. Yes, I been right here afore. And I know where we're at."

He said it like it was important.

And it was. Because we'd be bus riding and vegetable picking for what seemed to me to have been a heck of a dang time. Months and months and months. We never knowed where we were, and we were smart enough never to ask a crew boss. Mr. Boss didn't want us to know. He hated questions.

"When people don't know where they are, they're easy to harness. If they know, maybe they'll itch to run

64

away." That's how Coo Coo explain it. He didn't figure out everything. Just enough to spend out his life.

So when Coo Coo spring out of his bus seat, and pointed, and claimed that he knowed where we was at, I wanted to know, too.

"Where?"

"North of Pahokee."

My brain lit up like a Coleman lantern. Well, maybe not that brilliant, but at least like a wet smudge pot.

"Hey," I said, "I know about Pahokee."

"You do?"

"Honest. Miss Hoe said it was a place, a town, on Lake Okeechobee . . . like Jailtown or Clewiston or Moore Haven." I quit showing off my education long enough to take a breath. "So we gotta be close to Moore Haven, where I'm going . . . if I can ever figure how to scoot away to there."

"Easy," said Coo Coo.

"You want me to make Moore Haven, don't you?"

He nodded. "Yes, but wait until sundown, and you'll learn more, boy. A fact is worth something."

"What is it?"

"Sit patient. Sundown'll git here."

Waiting weren't easy right then.

After a while, we felt the bus stop and heard the familiar "Unload" order.

We didn't have to sleep in no bus that night. Instead, all us pickies got to stretch out on a shack floor, with straw. But it weren't very fresh. It'd been sleeped on by many a man and rolled into loose yellowy dust.

It beat a bus seat.

We got fed. Nothing special. Cold beans and green-edge bread and the customary company wine. I traded my bottle to Coo Coo for half his beans, which he sometimes give me anyhow. He said I was still growing and could use beans better than he could.

"In *you*," Coo Coo said, "them beans'll make into manhood." He laughed. "But inside *me*, they'll only blow a toot."

The sun final went down.

Coo Coo pointed at it like he was fixing to be certain I'd not miss seeing the sunset.

"Figure it out," he said.

The two of us sat on a half-log bench, our backs leaning against the picker shack. As we looked across Lake Okeechobee, the pink sunset set fire to the surface water, and burnt it all orange and pink.

"Sunset," said Coo Coo. "That's west."

"I don't get it."

"Moore Haven and Jailtown is clear across Okeechobee, boy. We ain't near at all to them westerly places. We's east."

My fists tightened as I looked westward toward home. A town where I was going to git to, or die trying. I could feel my letter tucked inside my shirt.

"I'm close enough," I said.

CHAPTER 12

It was luck.

Sometimes a event can't happen; yet then it up and do, the way a drifter could be really down on his luck, and trip across a four-leaf clover.

It leaped in my lap.

On the night that we camped north of Pahokee, in the shack with a straw floor, it stormed. Not merely a light rain. A heavy downpour. And with the rain there was lightning, very close, so nearby that the thunder didn't follow. Instead, it stepped on the thunder's toes. Both to once.

Coo Coo awoke. Getting up from his straw bed, he hobbled to the door where I was, to pull me back inside.

"Don't never," he warned me, "stand at a open doorway during a boomer. Them deadly bolts of electric juice'll seek a current. Any kind of a draft."

He holded me away from the door.

Inside our small shack was eight or nine others. Most of them was so wine drunk that they never bothered to stir, or crack an eye. Several was sick. One particular man might have been dead, or near it, yet I had no wanting to find out which.

"A person is dumber than a stump," Miss Binnie

Hoe used to tell us school kids, "unless he learns something every single day." Then she smiled and added, "and also every night."

Everything and everyone is a teacher, our little schoolmarm told us: All the happenings in our living, both the good and the evil, are tools to store away in the tool kit of the mind.

"Rain," I said to Coo Coo.

"What about it? Florida rain ain't nothing new."

Turning to him, I said something that I was more'n only partway sure of. "I'll bet Mr. Boss ain't outside in this rain."

Coo Coo grunted. "No, he probable ain't."

"And neither," I went on to say, "are any of his crew chiefs. Or the dogs. They're under a shelter somewhere, chinked into a place where they can't see squat or hear beans."

My old friend's eyes narrowed as he stared direct at me. For a few breaths, he didn't speak. Yet, by Coo Coo's face wrinkles, it was simple to tell there was something on his mind. He final let it out.

"Arly, you're up to mischief."

"If we're ever to git ourselfs away from this old worker gang," I said, "it'll be tonight."

"Git away . . . to what? I'm a picker. And it's all I know to do. How'll we eat?"

"I don't want to eat. Or have to. If'n I know that I'm actual going to Moore Haven, with my letter, and I don't guess I'll need as much as a pea."

Coo Coo stared out into the rain. "I run away before. They caught me. And they beat me with sugarcane stalks until they wasn't a place on me that weren't bleeding."

"You're afraid?"

Slowly he nodded. "Nobody never gits away, boy.

I been beat up, and cooned by dogs, half drown in a mule trough, branded, and rope dragged." He took a breath. "Yeah, I'm dang afraid."

"They won't catch us."

"Boy, do you realize how many times I've listen to a picker brag about that he'll never git caught?"

"No."

"Every time. On the night before they throw a rope on him, and drag him until he don't have a skin."

Around me, I could feel Roscoe Broda's rope, cutting into me. It was worse than dying.

"We can do it, Coo Coo. And even if we fail, we gotta try."

"I can't. He rested a hand on top of my shoulder. "Maybe *you* can."

"Tonight."

"You mean it?" he asked.

"Now," I told him. "Right now."

"How come *now?*"

"Coo Coo, I just recent told you. The rain. Every one of them catchers is under a roof. It's nighttime. They can't hear us, or sight us, or even come poking around with their lanterns and flashers to check on who's in what shack, or at another."

"The dogs'll track us, come light."

"No. They can't do it," I said. "Because the rain'll flush away the footmarks and all our smell."

Coo Coo shook his head. "Boy, them redbone hounds and blueticks can whiff a flea egg under a dead elephant."

"Oh, please go," I said. "When we git to Moore Haven, I know some people who'll take us in."

"Who? What's their name?" Coo Coo asked me.

"Bonner."

"Never heared of 'em."

I sighed. "They never hear of *you* either. But they heared of me. Miss Hoe wouldn't fib. I got a letter in my shirt."

"Let's see it."

Reaching for it, I pulled it out. Wet, but all mine. "See?"

Coo Coo snuffed and spat. "A whole lot of precious profit that'll afford you if'n the doggers catch us."

Outside, it seemed to sudden be raining harder.

"Let's go," I said.

"Now?"

"If'n we wait, we won't do it."

"How'll we git there?"

"Walk. It ain't any harder than picking."

"You don't know the way," he said.

"In my mind, I do. Miss Hoe showed us a map one time. An actual map."

"What of?"

"A map of Florida. It looked like a upside-down hitchhiker. Sort of a big thumb. She showed us that the large blue shape was Okeechobee. So, if'n we follow the lakeshore south, then west, we'll come to Moore Haven."

"Yeah," said Coo Coo, "we will eventual."

"I can't go without you," I said.

"And I won't let you go it lonesome."

"Will ya come?"

He nodded.

Right then, I wanted to throw both my arms around old Charles and hug him hard. In spite of his fears, and all of his hurting, he certain weren't a coward.

We shook hands.

Then, without even a look-behind, we run out the open doorway, into the rain and the night. It sure was coming down. We wouldn't care. Coo Coo and I were custom to a wetting, and had picked vegetables in rain more'n either one of us could total up.

Coming to a wire fence wasn't a promising sign.

But then, the two of us trotted along it, in search of a way over. We never found one. Yet I found a hole under. Some animal had dug it, pawed away the loose earth. It was dreadful muddy, but we crawled under that fence, spitted out the wet dirt, and run.

Along a sandy road, which by now weren't more than a muddy rut, Coo Coo and I come stumbling up on a stalled truck. It was still raining plentiful.

I could hear people talking.

Some ladies were chirping away, complaining, and I spotted a man's face behind the wheel. He was trying to git the truck engine to kick in. But no dice.

Peeking in the window on the driver's side, I saw a face, and it near to choke my breath.

It was Our Father John.

CHAPTER 13

"Holy Joe," said Coo Coo.

Our Father didn't notice us at first.

He was busy trying to handle controls and the wheel. Then he looked out his window. Cranking it down a inch or two, he squinted at us as we stood in the rain, and spoke.

"We don't have any money. We're a group of church people on the way to the poorhouse. But we just called my brother-in-law, Sheriff Cecil Lamberton, and he'll be here any minute. With guns and dogs."

"We don't want your money, sir," I said. "All we wanted to ask was . . . are y'all in trouble? If y'are, my friend and I might help out. Or push."

"Bless you, my dear friends. You have taken pity on us in our plight, and come to aid the Golden Prophets in this, our dire need."

Now, instead of frighted, his voice sounded close to being friendly.

"You in trouble?" I asked.

"Yes, my son. However, perhaps all we require is a healthy heave by a pair of strong field workers, and we shall be merrily on our way." He made a slight frown. "That is, if I can ever get this contraption to start."

"It's a miracle," Coo Coo said.

I turned around to him. "What is?"

"Boy, we can strike up a deal. A exchange. If'n we scratch Holy Joe's back, he'll scratch ours."

"You mean . . . beg a ride to Moore Haven?"

"Or," said Coo Coo, "to any wherever Mr. Boss ain't."

"Our Father," I said, "we'd like to offer you a push." He smiled. "If," I added, "you can give us a lift."

The Holy Joe stopped smiling. "We may not be going your way," he said. "If we were, I assure both of you that the Golden Prophets would hasten to oblige."

"Does that mean *no?*" I asked.

"It ain't a *yes,*" Coo Coo said. "Mister, we are sorry to tell ya, but it's your misfortune that Arly and me maybe ain't *pushing* your way."

"We don't have enough room in our truck. Why, there's barely room enough for ourselves, say nothing about . . . about strangers."

"If we push," I said, "we'll be friends."

Holy Joe sighed. But then he smiled. "Oh, very well. I guess we would owe you both a ride. Providing, of course, you people can push us." He laughed. "And even if you can't, we can make the room to take you in."

Coo Coo examined the truck wheels that were rutted in mud. "The rain'll soon rinse the muck off the road. Be patient."

"How long will it be?" Our Father asked.

Coo Coo shrugged.

Our Father John Patrick Mulligan, even with the help of his bestowed title plus the constant advice of all the impatient Sisters, couldn't start the truck. It stood in the rain.

So did Coo Coo and I.

The driver window got cranked up again, to a full close, yet I could hear a ample of talk from the inside. Most all of it was Sisterly nagging at Our Father on how to start a truck engine. The truck seemed not to be a cab and a cargo van, but all one unit. One room. The more the Sisters all cackled, the steamier the truck window glass become.

They sure puffed up a fog.

As the Sisters complained, and advised, Holy Joe seemed to sink lower and lower behind the wheel, as though he was actual in a swamp mire.

Standing outside in the rainstorm, Coo Coo and I commenced to enjoy the free show, like it was a circus. Inside, the Holy Joe was starting to look wetter (and worse off) than we was. Every voice in the vehicle seemed to have a opinion, and each viewpoint was being aired with a blend of passion and volume.

"All right," I thought I'd overhear Our Father surrender to say. "Oh, all right." The window rolled down a inch again. "Upon discussion," Our Father announced, "the Golden Prophets have voted to include the two of you, to welcome you into our entourage."

"Zat mean we ride?" Coo Coo asked.

"Yes. If we manage to move this Satanic invention, you have my solemn word the two of you shall join us, and move along with it. Furthermore, we will try to escort you to wherever it is you're going. Even if it's a bit out of our way."

My luck held.

Beneath the tires, the mud did eventual rinse away, leaving more solid ground. And the Holy Joe, summoning all of his spiritual and mechanical wisdom, coaxed the engine to turn over.

It started. We pushed, and then rode.

Up front, behind the wheel, sat our leader by his lonesome. But everyone else (all females) wanted to stay in the main section of the truck, and stare at Coo Coo and me. Nobody spoke a word. All the Sisters done was glare at us, eyeing our soaking wet clothes, and say nary a thing. They probable thought we was criminals.

The truck was packed full of clothes, folded cots, a few small trunks, musical instruments, and boxes, each of which bore the same label: BIBLES

None of the Sisters, I took notice, was old.

No gray hair. All young, and mostly pretty. I wondered if they were the daughters of Our Father. I doubted it, seeing no family favoring in looks.

The youngest and prettiest seemed to be about my age. I didn't know her name, nor she mine. Yet, as the truck plowed forward through a long rainy night, the girl would steal a glance at me. When she appeared to think that none, or few, of the other Sisters would observe, she winked.

Finally, one of the growed-up Sisters took a note of the eye activity, and whispered a warning that I could hear.

"Delilah, you stop."

So that was the pretty girl's name. Delilah. I wondered if she owned a second name, like mine was Poole. Delilah kept winking at me, and I had to admit that I don't guess I was objecting too much. Her smile was a dessert.

"You're still doing it, Delilah."

"Doing what, Sister?"

"I keep seeing you winking at that hitchhiker boy."

"I'm sure sorry. But it's not a wink. It righteous is a twitch. That's what the doctor called it. A twitchy eye."

"Righteous has nothing to do with it, Delilah, and

I wouldn't refer to your on-purpose wink as a twitch. I'd call it outright *flirty.*"

"Yes'm."

Beside me, his back to a BIBLE crate, Coo Coo was asleep, snoring, and again mumbling his affections for Hattie.

As the truck chugged on through the rain and darkness, one by one, all of the Golden Prophet Sisters fell asleep. All, except one. Delilah was awake. So was I. It wasn't easy (maybe impossible) for a boy to fall asleep when a girl is staring in his direction.

A pretty girl that winked.

Maybe it was a nervous twitch. All I knowed was this. Her looking at me, winking, had started my nerves to jangle, more than a mite, and before I could control myself, it happened! My right eye winked at Delilah.

Perhaps it was merely a blink, not a wink, but Delilah's face brighted up quick. Her winker eye fired off three rapid-fire rounds.

Wink. Wink. Wink.

Then come the big surprise. The whopper. Delilah pretended to kiss me. Eyes closed, she puckered her lips into a sweet little rosebud kiss, even though we never touched. And made a sucking noise. With one hand, she motioned for me to come to her, and sit beside her. Moving some, she made room.

So I leaped like a spring frog.

"What's your name?" Delilah asked.

"Arly," I told her. "Arly Poole."

Wink.

"Mine is Delilah." She leaned her face closer to mine. "Don't you think that's a pretty name?"

"Yes," I whispered.

"So is Arly. And you're a pretty boy." Her finger

touched my hand. "And I just *love* pretty boys. And I'd guess you'd fancy a pretty girl."

I nodded.

"Do you think I'm pretty, Arly Poole?"

"Yes'm, I do. I certain do." As I said so, I could feel my face heating up enough to fry eggs.

"Tomorrow, I can look a ample lot prettier when I don't have to be inside this old black dress."

She kissed my ear.

It was a wet kiss. Almost warm water.

"Is . . . is the Our Father gentleman your pa?"

She pulled away. "Him? Shucks no. My cousin Ruth Louise joined up with the Golden Prophets . . . she's the one over there with her hair in braids . . . and she talked me into joining, too." Delilah giggled. "You and your old friend can't join the Prophets. You won't be allowed."

"How come?"

"Our Father only takes in females. See for yourself," she said, with a gesture of her hand. "All ladies. Each and every lady's as saintly as I am." She slapped her leg, and then mine.

Right then, before I could say anything else, she kissed me full on the mouth. It wasn't what anybody'd label a holy doing. Much like the sudden kick of a mule, it got my full attention. Her kiss sort of wandered all over my face.

Like it wanted to be lost.

And found.

CHAPTER 14

Coo Coo laughed.

"Well," he said, "I'm final dry."

As it turned out, Coo Coo didn't quite foretell what Our Father (the Holy Joe) and all the Golden Prophets of Salvation had in store for his betterment.

Earlier that morning, when the truck come gasping to a quit, Coo Coo had been questioned by Our Father John as to whether or not he had ever got baptized. The Sisters, as well as the Holy Joe, all seemed to be curious as to Coo Coo's spiritual state of grace.

"Me?" Coo Coo shook his head. "*No,* not me."

It was a wrong answer. Right sudden, they all also asked me the same, but I smelt what was coming next, and spouted out a whopper:

"Oh, yes indeed," I lied. "I was baptized in the sacred flowing waters of the Lord, by the Reverend Brother Smith, who was our pastor at home."

From that moment on, all attention seemed to zero in on poor Coo Coo, an unwashed, whose soul now lay in harm's way. All the Golden Prophets were eyeing Coo Coo as though he'd been hogtied on the tracks of a railroad to Perdition, and ol' red Lucifer hisself was the engineer at the throttle of a onrushing locomotive of transgression.

"Assist him," said Our Father.

At the time, all us Golden Prophets of Salvation had made camp neighborly to a river bank, close to Belle Glade.

"Seize the sinner."

I certain had to give old Coo Coo credit, because he fought those Sisters and their assisting more fierce than a jungle tiger. But he was old and they were young. Coo Coo was outnumbered. And outgunned.

"Help me," Coo Coo cried. "Don't let these Christers have their way with me. Save me, Arly . . . save me."

"You *shall* be saved," said Our Father.

During the entire tussle, Our Father John stood stiller than a statue, and calmly smiled. To him, a sinner was a sinner, and today's target was presently getting hauled, body and soul, toward a handy stream.

Coo Coo swore.

Nothing fancy. Yet a work of art, even though it was just a long string of old favorites, for close to half a minute, without repeat. It was close to poetry.

Holy Joe, however, pretended not to hear.

"Vituperation," he intoned, using his sermon voice, "shall not benefit you, Brother Coo Coo." He turned quick to me. "What," he asked me, "is the proper name of this baptismal candidate?"

"You mean Coo Coo's name?"

"Yes, my son. What is it? Tell me."

"Charles."

By now, Charles, and a half a dozen of the Sisters, were now locked in combat in knee-deep *living* (flowing to the sea) water. Never did I suspect that Coo Coo was able put up so salty a sporting. Yet he did. Fighting tooth and nail (in his case, mostly nails), my old buddy dug in, to stage a final stand.

Almost a year ago, Miss Hoe had described a battle scene to us. Now, before my eyes, "the valiant hero [her terms] nearly managed to ward off the attackers who surrounded him, inflicting mortal wounds on all flanks."

As I watched, Coo Coo become Custer.

There he stood, firing profanity from a hot barrel, amidst a circle of *unpainted* warriors, all of whom intended to conquer sin. And pickers.

To my surprise, Our Father John Patrick Mulligan now removed his shining black footwear and black stockings, and waded triumphantly into the river. A Moses crossing the Jordan. Or whoever crossed it. Maybe it was only Hannibal crossing Missouri.

Safe on shore, I smiled.

Coo Coo happened to see me smiling, shook a fist, and voiced such a vile threat that even the Devil, had he been present, would certain have muffed his ears.

"Arly," he hooted, "you dang filthy son of a . . ."

Under he was plunged.

"Never," old Brother Smith had once advised Huff Cooter and me, "belittle the potent Almighty or the might of the faithful."

Watching, I had no grasp of the power of the Lord Above, yet it was plain to see just how powerful, and persisting, the Sisterly Golden Prophets of Salvation could be. Whatever they lacked in size, they certain made up in spunk.

Coo Coo's head was dunked.

Not once.

Not twice.

But three times.

Each dunking of our baptismal candidate seemed to

make Our Father John happier and happier. *Sin,* he was witnessing, was being scoured away, in a current where it never would return to plague this lowly unfortunate field picker with temptations of the flesh, wine bottle, or poker cards.

"Hattie," I said, "I wish you were here."

It was plain to see. The dirtier the sinner, the more dunking he needed in order to cleanse his immortal soul (these were all terms I was currently sponging in from our Holy Joe) and to preserve his eternal virtue . . . until he was final prepared to climb the Golden Stairs and enter Kingdom's Hall.

I'd never soaked up religion in such a hefty helping. My celestial plate was filled, and refilled, until I was busting with righteousness, abrim with Amen.

Coo Coo, meanwhile, must have certain been drowning, as his face had gotten pushed under (and held under) to combat each and every sin that could tempt any human being, domestic or foreign.

Never, before that day, did I realize that anyone, not even a aging wino, could stay beneath the water for so long a period, and still cuss. Even though Coo Coo's oathing come up in the form of bubbles. The worse he cussed, the more Our Father baptized.

Religion bested rage.

After a good hour, when each of Coo Coo's lungs had inhaled at least a gallon of river water, the Saved Soul was escorted ashore, blessed, prayed over, and finally revived.

"Bless you, Charles," said Our Father.

Blessing or not, Coo Coo's temper did manage to dampen and fall a degree or two. Once dry, Charles may not have acted too saintly, but he did appear (and smell) a lot neater.

The Holy Joe actual asked Coo Coo whether or not

he intended to purchase a Bible, one with "Golden Prophets of Salvation" imprinted on its *genuine leatherette* cover. Coo Coo telled him sudden soon that he didn't cotton to buy even as much as a penny dreadful.

In a way, however, both Coo Coo and I actual did become part of the Golden Prophets.

We weren't paid in money.

Yet we each got given a new secondhand shirt and some trousers (no shoes) to wear. This wasn't charity. Coo Coo and I earned our keep, doing odd jobs, setting up the tent, and unloading the truck. We were fed. The food was usual hot and wholesome (no stale bread, and for certain *no wine*) and we always got a slab of pie. In a town, Our Father stopped the truck and bought Delilah and me some strawberry ice cream.

Best of all, no picking.

Our big chance at stardom come, just by luck, during one of our evening Revival meetings. Our Father John called for sinners to come forward. But, for the very first time, the entire congregation of twenty people held ground. No one come.

That's when Coo Coo seemed to sense a problem, so he stepped forward. Our Father was both surprised and pleased.

"On your knees," he ordered Coo Coo, who obliged. "Bow your head, sinner, and confess your sin to Jehovah."

Kneeling and facing the crowd, Coo Coo confessed.

"Dice," he yelled up at Heaven, eyes closed tight in total devotion. "I hung out at pool parlors and racetracks. Not to mention all the poker and rummy and . . . and . . . Spit in the Ocean."

"Do you repent, my son?"

"*Yes*," howled Coo Coo, managing to keep a sober

face. "Our Father, you won't find me within no mile of a pool table from this day forward, or my name isn't . . . Ace King."

"Rise," commanded Our Father John, "rise to your feet, Mr. King, and praise the Lord for making you clean. You've been *reborn*."

"Praise the Lord," Coo Coo hooted out.

"Amen," said the Sisters.

That was the moment when I decided that if Coo Coo could become a tent star, anybody could. Even me. As there was a strange piece of old wood nearby, I grabbed it, shoved it under a armpit, and limped forward for all to witness.

"Grandpa," I whimpered to Coo Coo, "be it true you won't fix to gamble no more? You ain't going to fritter your money away to all those greedy card sharpies? Tell me it's true, Grandpa, so we can have bread on our table. And . . . and that we'll save up enough money to pay a doctor, and I can final have my . . . my operation . . . and *walk* again."

Women wept.

Men honked noses.

Cash dumped into Our Father's black hat like never before. Not only pennies and nickels. Several kicked in a *whole dollar!* But among all those who witnessed my music-hall performance, one person was so special pleased.

Delilah.

Coo Coo be true worried.

"Boy," he kept telling me, "when a picker high-
tails away from a field crew, there's usual a reward for
people who'll help to haul him back."

He didn't trust a single solitary one of the Golden
Prophets of Salvation, not even our leader.

"You mean," I asked him, "that Holy Joe himself
would turn us over to Mr. Boss, for the bounty fee?"

Coo Coo spat. "Most of the Holy Joes I met would
sell their mother, father, sister, dog, or grandmother for
a dime. And probable deliver all five for a quarter."

The following evening, Coo Coo and I performed
again. His gambling sin. My gimpy fakery, complete
with crying and wood under my arm. Our Father
discarded the stick I'd earlier used, sharpened a knife,
and carved me a new crutch, adding a soft mound of
padding for under my arm.

It worked a wonder.

For the bigger shows, at which sometimes even half
a hundred hopefuls would attend, seeking to be Saved,
our repentance act would have three actors, instead of
two.

Delilah posed as my blind sister.

Our finale was more than even the hardest of hearts could bear. Coo Coo (the gambling, dice-rolling, pool-shooting, card-cheating no-good) continued to serve as *our opening overture,* as Our Father John called it. Then I limped forward on a crutch, trailed by our clincher, little blind Delilah, who groped her sightless way to embrace both Coo Coo and me.

A family united . . . and Saved.

Salvation.

Never before did I realize that there was so much human *saliva* in Salvation.

Whenever we put on our tent show Revival Meeting, there was somebody who'd sink to the ground and foam at the mouth. This was a happening that never seemed to upset Our Father John Patrick Mulligan. Instead, he appeared to revel in spit. The more the foam, the more heated come the fervor of his sermon.

At the first foaming fleck, Our Father would hasten to the stricken attendee, fall to his knees, circle his arms around the person, and loudly praise the Lord.

I didn't know exact why. But, night after night, I started to believe what our Holy Joe was preaching. It took me a spell to understand. Final, it come. The reason I begun to believe Our Father John was because *he* believed in God. John Patrick Mulligan was becoming a Christian.

Whenever things went wrong, and it was certain that something would go awry, Our Father became less upset, and more helpful. In my eyes, Holy Joe was *our father* in aplenty of ways. Whenever a Sister didn't feel up to snuff, Our Father John no longer urged the infirmed one to perform at our Revival.

"Ladies," he told me in private, "are different than us gentlemen. Their bodies are quite unique, Arly, and someday you will discover this for yourself. I mean in wedlock, naturally."

"How so different?"

He sighed.

"You are still so young. Please don't think that you must learn, or discover, everything there is to know in one year. How old are you, Arly?"

I didn't know.

"I used to be eleven."

He smiled. "Perhaps now you're twelve. From the size and height of you, yes, I'd say twelve years might be accurate enough."

"What are you telling me?"

"Just so. Soon, our sweet Delilah will no longer be a child. Certain changes will take place within her. They, I believe, are called cycles. Her inner chemistry will change." He laughed. "We fellows don't experience such a phenomenon. But our lady friends do."

"What sort of changes?"

"Sometimes our friend Delilah will be ill at ease. Then, at other times, she might become unruly, or tense, and even snap at you, and at the other Sisters."

"I don't understand."

Our Father smiled. "Neither," he said softly, "do I. Yet I'd imagine that a gentleman was never intended, by God, to fully understand all of the varieties of a female's mood." He placed a hand gently atop my head, mussing my hair. "When it occurs, please know that you, Arly, are not its cause. It is merely Mother Nature, in her way, and in her artistic variety."

"How'll I know?"

"Her hand may seek her stomach. Delilah may be in discomfort. I believe," he whispered, "it's called *cramps*."

"Oh."

"Remember this. When ladies have a stomachache, it is a gentleman's duty to be gentle and forgiving. Later on, her forgiveness of your particular shortcomings will be offered in full measure." Lowering his voice again, Our Father added, "Above all, when these so-called cramps take place, do not ask personal questions. Pretend you don't even notice."

Each day I'd watch Delilah.

At any minute, I expected her to clutch her belly, fall to earth, and faint away into a cycle, or bicycle, or even a tricycle if it suited her. Nothing like such took place. But, I noticed that one of our Sisters was complaining about cramps, holding her middle, and saying something about a *curse*.

Well, as good old Coo Coo would usual say, it was certain as shooting all Greek to me.

Our Father also noticed her. He looked direct at me, lifted his eyebrows, and then approached me in a most fatherly fashion.

"Cycle," he whispered, twirling a little circle in the air with a chubby finger.

Then he winked at me, as though the pair of us shared a secret that only three folks knowed. Our Father John and Mother Nature and me.

I thought about all this cycle stuff for a few days. It made me trust Father John. Coo Coo, however, felt to the contrary.

"He's a fake," Coo Coo insisted, speaking of Our Father.

"No," I said. "He actual ain't."

"Our show's nothing except a phony fake."

"Well," I agreed, "part of it's hokum. A sideshow. But his feelings about God, the feelings that he doesn't really share with any of us, are as real as rain, Coo Coo. Honest. He loves God. And more, Our Father John loves all of us. Every single doggone man-jack of us." I grinned. "Even you."

Coo Coo shook his head. "Arly, I'm maybe too olden to believe in anything. Or believe in any person. Or any Lord."

"Then," I said, "I feel sorry for you."

He frowned. "I don't want no pity, boy."

"No. Neither do I. All I'm asking is that you give old Holy Joe a break. Outside, he's a slicker. Inside, he's good."

The two of us were sitting on a pair of turpentine barrels, outside a produce shed, near a town I didn't know. It was early morning. None of the Golden Prophets of Salvation had ever worked even one single day as a field hand. At dawn, none of them did anything except roll over and slumber.

Coo Coo and I were usual first up.

And awake. Trying to scare out a breakfast.

We were eating right good. Business was flowering. The Golden Prophets of Salvation were saving souls right and left, and they certain had saved old Ace King and Arly Poole. We even got our truck engine repaired enough to start on the fifth or sixth try.

I felt prospering.

Almost a pound fatter.

Delilah even remarked that I was adding a ample lot of muscle, and that I would soon sprout up skyward, to be taller than she was measuring.

Looking up, I saw her coming toward me. Coo Coo was friend enough to leave, and limped away. It felt nifty to be alone with Delilah, and just be two kids.

I asked Delilah where we was at. She didn't know. But then hurried off to inquire of Our Father John, and then returned, smiling.

"La Belle," she said.

The name didn't sound as though I'd know exact where we'd be. Certain not where we was heading.

"Why," she asked me, "do you want to know?"

Before answering, I held quiet. No sense in telling Delilah that I was fixing to jump ship as soon as we'd locate close to Moore Haven.

As she sat beside me, I moved a inch or two closer to her, almost baking in the warmth of her nearness. We'd become more than sweethearts. Delilah and I were friends. And I knowed that nothing, or nobody, could ever change what we had. It belonged to only us.

Everyone else in our group was a grownup person. All except Delilah and me.

We were the only two people who walked together holding hands. And whenever Our Father John would mention *love* in one of his sermons, Delilah would look direct at me. I'd always do a likewise.

Right now, she was smiling at me. Her smile had a way of almost kissing my face with gentleness. It seemed I knowed her always.

"Delilah, what month are we in?"

"September. It's September, 1928."

"Are you sure?"

"Yes," she said, giving my lips a gentle kiss. "And pleasant things always happen in September. I ought to know, Arly Poole."

"What sort of pleasant things?"

"September's my birthday."

CHAPTER 16

"Saturday night," Coo Coo said.

We were helping three of the Sisters wallop the dishes, pots, and frypans, following a filling supper of pork ribs, collards with vinegar, fresh hot biscuits with a few raisins. Plus a giant whale of a watermelon, and a baked apple for every soul of us.

"What," I asked Coo Coo, "is so special about Saturday night? It sort of favors any other, don't it?"

"Years back, Hattie and me used to step a dance sometimes. A fancy clog. Or we'd fetch ourselfs out on a date."

"What's today's date, Coo Coo?"

He looked at me, handing me a pot to towel dry, soap all over his hands and arms. "Why do you sudden care what the date is? You planning to attend some sort of a social?"

"No."

"Maybe," he sort of sang in order to torment me a mite, "you got designs to do a socializer with our little Miss Delilah and her batty green eyes."

"Maybe I do."

He handed me a saucepan. "Okay, then, how come you be so curious about what the date is?"

"Her birthday's in September, and that's the month we're in right now. But I don't guess I know which day of September today righteous is."

"Ask the Holy Joe."

"Will he know?"

"Yup. It's a part of accounting up the profits for the Prophets."

When I located him, behind the truck wheel, I asked Our Father John about the date.

"Saturday," he told me. "Today is Saturday, my boy, the fifteenth day of September, in the year of our Lord, 1928."

"Tomorrow," I said.

Our Father stared at me. "What about it?"

"It's the sixteenth of September."

"And that's special?" he asked.

"Yes, sir, it sure is."

"Why?"

I looked at the ground. "It's Delilah's birthday."

He smiled. "Ah," he said, closing the Bible that he had been studyin', "I must be thick. Of course. It is our fair Delilah's birthday. And it shall be a date for you to remember, Arly. So please do. Because it will be the first birthday of Delilah's that you'll be here to celebrate. The sixteenth day of September, in the year 1928."

"I ought to give her a present."

"Indeed."

"But I don't have any money to buy it."

He stepped out of the truck, and hopped down, grunting. Prosperity, even though recent, had added a pound or two on our leader.

"Arly," he said, "all gifts do not originate in a store. Perhaps the best gifts are those that nobody can wrap in shiny paper. We don't need to tie a fancy pink bow on friendship, or trust, or the Christianity with which we favor one another."

I smiled. "I'd plan to give her candy."

His eyebrows raised. "Sweets to the sweet?"

"Sort of."

He said, "Then perhaps I can muster our forces to a near victory." Disappearing inside the truck once again, he was gone for a spell, then returned. I expected that he was searching for candy. Not a whole lot of it. Just a jellybean, or gumdrop. But what he was carrying couldn't be eaten.

"Here," he said, "is a radio."

He handed it to me. I was a bit surprised how heavy it was. The radio was brown wood, humpbacked, with little metal knobs in front, below the cloth. Dangling from it was a electric cord. And a plug.

Our Father smiled. "Inside our truck," he said, "I hired a mechanic to hook up a special whatever-it-is, and it'll play a radio. From the truck battery. I tried it. And it really operates and uses up very little juice."

"Wow," I said. "I never heared a radio before. From a distant. But not up close."

"About time. Let's test it."

We tested it.

The radio wouldn't play right away quick.

"It has to warm up," Our Father said. "Then we can listen to some boop-boop-a-doop singer." He giggled at his little joke.

As the radio was warming, Our Father John fiddled with the two knobs. "Now I recall," he said. The dial on the left . . . listen to it go *click click* . . . is what turns the radio on and off. But this one over here, to the right, selects the radio station that the listener prefers. It doesn't go *click* at all."

Hearing something, Our Father and I leaned in

close. It weren't music. Just a long, steady, prickly sound. Working the left button made the noise louder, then softer, and final disappear.

"What's that noise?"

"It's static."

"Do people listen to that?"

"No." He laughed good-naturedly. "What they listen to mostly is advertising. Somebody trying to huckster something to somebody else to wash with a certain soap used by the Hollywood flicker stars."

I'd heared about Hollywood, near Miami.

A light began to turn orange on the little dial window. Our Father seemed to be pleased about it.

"What do that light mean?" I asked.

"It means the radio is warming to its task. Now, we work the selection dial, as soon as I can tone the static down to a whisper, and perhaps we can find something worth listening to, besides a pitch to drink Coca-Cola."

I heard a human voice. It made me jump, because it seemed there was a little man inside the radio, and he was shouting out, right through the pretty brocade cloth. We could hear some words, but not many. Mostly it was nothing but a lot of that stuff called static.

"This is strange," said Our Father. "Very strange. I can usually locate two or three stations that can deliver music on this contraption."

Again we heard the man's voice: "Florida (static) storm warning (static) shelter . . . storm (static and more static) heavy rain predicted. Fierce winds up to . . . (static) damage in Puerto Rico."

Our Father looked at me stern. "Arly, now don't pester me why, but I suspect something is seriously wrong somewhere. And it has to do with all of our recent rainy weather."

"Honest?"

He nodded. "Go fetch Delilah and bring her back here to the truck. I'm going to ask the pair of you to be . . . radio sentinels, if you will."

I ran.

When Delilah and I returned, Our Father John was still twisting the two little knobs. A needle on the dial was swinging back and forth. The radio wasn't producing anything except the crackling noise. Not a note of music.

"Delilah," said Our Father, "how would you and Arly like to sit up here on the driver's seat and listen to the radio?"

"Oh," she said, "we would like it a lot."

I nodded.

"This radio listening is Arly's birthday present to you," said Our Father, "and mine too. But I do expect you to remain alert, and awaken me if you happen to hear any important news. You can pretend it's a *game* and *you* are the watchdogs."

He left.

I worked the radio, pretending to be a real broadcasting expert, in order to impress Delilah. But I don't guess a boy can win a girl's affection with nothing but static. As I was about to give up I struck gold. My dialing happened to hit on a music station, but the music was so faint that the station must've been up on the moon.

Best of all was that our faces touched as we was both so close to the radio's cloth.

The songs were toe tappers:

"If You Knew Susie."

"Avalon."

"Sleepy Time Gal."

"Five Foot Two, Eyes of Blue."

"Love Nest."

94

"Look for the Silver Lining."

"Whispering."

It weren't all steady music. Some of it was more static than songs, but Delilah and I held hands, hugged, and kissed. For a good long spell, we were about the world's two happiest watchdogs.

Until the station went dead.

A song had just quit playing, and a tired-sounding man was saying, ". . . Rising water . . . weather bureau report . . . (static) . . . telephone lines all down . . . destroying the city of West Palm Beach . . ."

Delilah and I got bored with all that crackly noise, so we turned the radio complete off.

It was more fun to love.

The best part was when Delilah said, "Arly, we didn't need a radio to be happy. But thank you. The way I truly feel is that my best birthday present is knowing a boy as sweet as you."

I couldn't say a word. So I just did what I felt like doing.

Kissing each freckle on her face.

CHAPTER 17

We slept.
 During the night, it rained. As a picker, I'd seen
rain before, but nothing at all like this. Outside the
truck, there didn't seem to be any empty space.

Only the wind and the water.

Delilah and I had been lucky enough to roll the
truck windows all the way up to tight before we fell
asleep. Now the glass was total steamy. Neither she nor
I could look out to see anything at all.

Bang.

Something hard and heavy hit the truck roof. We
both jumped. Then the ceiling of the truck sprung a
couple of leaks; one a small trickle, the other a river.

"Something is real wrong," Delilah said.

I agreed. When I tried to open the truck door, the
wind hammered it shut. The other door wouldn't even
budge. Delilah was screaming something, but I had no
prayer of hearing what it was.

The wind was punishing the truck.

Never, not in my whole life, had I ever heared noise
like this. Delilah and I were yelling at one another,
inside the truck, but no words come out. The glass
cracked to a shatter, and a busted-off tree limb punched

inside the cab, looking like one wounded finger of a drowning giant's hand.

Following the tree limb and the pieces of glass come the water. It wasn't merely rain. I saw solid water entering our truck and there wasn't much to breathe, only leaves and dirt. The water poured in a muddy brown. Not empty water. It was filled with all kinds of trash. And tasted salty.

It all come through the window. Mud, somebody's rubber boot, and a dead bird.

Wham.

Again an object crashed into our truck and I felt the whole vehicle turning over. As it landed on its side, the door ripped off; so I climb out, pulling Delilah with me.

"Hang tight to me," I tried to yell to her.

No words. Only the noise.

Before I could get a better grip on Delilah, she was gone. She just wasn't there anymore. Gone. There was no use trying to see, or hear, because all there be was water.

"Delilah!"

Forcing my eyes open, I saw a massive wall of solid water coming at me. It was water on top of water, and this wave was about as tall as a house. It swept in. There was no light, and even under all that water I could still hear the roaring crashing noise.

I couldn't breathe.

"Delilah . . ."

My head slammed into something hard and it hurt to the point of some awful sickness. I felt dizzy, upside down, and my supper vomited out my mouth and nostrils.

There was nothing to see.

Water. Wind. Noise without letup. Noise that kept

pounding on me, and beating me, making me beg it all to stop.

I wanted Coo Coo, or Our Father.

I needed someone, or something to hang onto, to hold . . . somebody I know. A person I could recognize. But I had nothing. All the world was a muddy browny gray, and little light. A lot of loose stuff. In my mouth the water didn't taste sweet and cool, like water ought. Instead it tasted like cold dirty death. It wouldn't stop. Fighting, I managed to poke my head up above the water's surface. Biting rain and whipping wind. And noise, noise, noise. It sounded like all the loud noises of the world were mixed into one screeching, scraping scream. Even under the water. Up, under, then up again.

My body smashed into a building, twisting into some sort of a corner. I hung on, trying to grab anything. And I did find something. Squinting, I saw what it was. A human arm. No body. Only a naked arm and hand. The arm looked bad busted and there was no color. It had already bled to a dead white.

"Coo Coo!"

Because I could sudden breathe, I shouted. Yet not a sound came out of my mouth. No name, no Coo Coo, no Delilah, and no leader.

"Our Father . . . Our Father John."

While I was trying to holler, the water come again, serpenting around the corner of a tall shed, a giant phython of moving, endless power. It hit. With a deep strangling death that filled my lungs, my nose, eyes, and ears, my mouth that was working so hard to shout, to breathe.

My fingers catched on to something. As the water washed away, for a moment, I saw what I was clutching.

A dead dog.

For an instant, it looked like one of the tracker

hounds owned by Mr. Boss. A bluetick or a redbone. The dog didn't appear to have any shape. Its bones must've been mostly cracked, because it flowed limp, like swamp weed. My hands tried to release their grip in the dog hair, but couldn't, as though my fingers was hooked into the animal's hide.

My head went under again, beneath the tons of raging water.

My mind saw faces: Miss Hoe, and Brother Smith. He looked like God, as usual. Big and strong and gentle, because he was smiling. I could read the dead faces of Huff Cooter and his pretty sister, Essie May Cooter. I saw the fancy social ladies at the Lucky Leg, in Jailtown, and the lady who held the boss job there, Miss Angel Free.

I saw all of Shack Row.

And my daddy. Dan Poole.

I wanted to pray that Essie May Cooter wouldn't die, and wouldn't drown. That she could escape from the Lucky Leg Social Palace, and not have to entertain the dandy gentlemen, or the dredgers who'd come to buy a kiss, upstairs in the bedrooms.

A loose tree come along.

Trees didn't move. They stood up tall, in one place, rooted deep in the dirt of Florida. Yet here it be, a ferny cypress, floating toward me, on top.

It come. I grabbed on.

Though the snubbed-off branches cut at my face, I manage to grip a purchase on the tree. It floated. A tree was all wood and it couldn't sink, not even if the water become a hundred foot deeper.

As my fingernails bit to the bark, I could smell, and taste, the for-sure cypress aroma. Strong. Old as the swamp itself. A Florida smell.

"Coo Coo! Delilah! Our Father John!"

I wanted Coo Coo safe from the water. So much of it, I figured as I clung to the cypress branches, had to be nothing except old Okeechobee. There weren't so much water anywhere else. I'd growed up beside it, in Jailtown. Okeechobee water was a lake. It looked sweet, and it tasted sweeter. But the water that I was now coughing up, puking out, weren't anything at all like our Lake Okeechobee.

It carried a sting to it. Sharp and mean and not fit to swallow, or cook with, or wash in, or baptize. Not a lake, a sea.

It was salt.

More water come. Much more than before. With it come the wind, a devil whirlwind that lashed everything into splinters and mud and cold wet death.

For a while, as I was a part of my floating uprooted cypress tree, I counted the dead bodies. One, a black lady. Two, a very skinny man who was naked, except for one brown stocking on a white and lifeless leg. Three, a redhaired child, so young that I'd not knowed whether it be a girl or a boy.

Only a child.

After a bit, I had to quit counting. An old man washed by me, almost close enough for me to reach out and rescue, and I tried. But then his open-mouth face sunk below the surface. I couldn't grab his hand that was the only part of him still above water.

He sunk.

My heart sunk with him.

Dead animals everywhere.

I saw mules, goats, kittens, more dogs, a cow, large birds and small, parakeets, an ibis, a spoonbill, and a flock of storks. All dead.

I noticed a dead Seminole. His face seemed to say . . . "This is Florida, my home, and I understand."

Even a hurricane.

CHAPTER 18

I floated with the tree.

No way of telling for how long, or how far. Only my face was above the water. Not all the time. Waves kept coming to wash over me.

Beneath my bare feet, I felt nothing but water. It was deep, a current that pulled and sucked at my legs and body. Water, water, wind, and rain. There was nothing to see. So, for a good lot of the time, I kept my eyes shut tight. Holding on. Clutching until my fingers seemed to be cramped into a lock on the small swaying branch.

Objects kept striking my head.

Some was soft.

Other stuff was hard. Nothing of the same size. All different. A car tire, small trees, a large citrus box, and many lengths of loose boards and timbers. A wooden chair. A child's rag doll. Plus a million splinters.

Everything was loose. Nothing together, except for the endless water. All of Florida seemed to be separated into pieces. Hunks of junk. All of it angry and churning.

The world was coming apart.

"Coo Coo . . ."

My voice made no sound.

"Delilah?"

Water and wind and unending noise.

Then it stopped!

Blinking rapid, I could see. No land. Only a cypress tree and my own arm, but overhead, a hole in the storm. A actual hole clear up through the wet gray to the sky. No sun. I watched as the giant eye passed over my head moving westward.

I could final hear my own voice yelling for Our Father John and Delilah and Coo Coo.

The strange quiet didn't last.

Again the storm renewed, with more windy rain, and also along come the thundering noise that weren't really thunder; it was the wind whipping my loose cypress tree around as if it weren't nothing more than a tore-up weed. I whipped with it. Not trusting my fingers to stay tight to their grip, I bit a twig, feeling my teeth cut into the bark.

It was dark again.

Almost black.

I wanted to cry because I felt so weak, oh so tired, very afraid. And alone. When a mule floated into me, I wanted to scream for help, feeling a dead hoof kicking at my lower body. As quick as the drowned mule had come, it left. It went on and on and on. The rain continued. But then the sky lightened and the wind didn't seem to be blowing quite as hard. I could see, and make out most of my tree.

I head a faint noise.

Squinting, I could see something move about twenty feet from where I was holding on to a branch with only my face above water.

The noise repeated. A *mew*.

Then I saw a cat. It looked dead, but dead cats don't do noise. And this animal did. The cat was so wet that it appeared to be nothing except a face, four legs, and almost no body at all.

With my body staying in the water, I worked my way, branch to branch, to where the cat had now slipped and fallen into the surging current. I grabbed it. Claws pricked into my hand as the cat screeched, but I held it close, until I could position it on the cypress trunk near my face.

The little cat was female.

"Cat," I said.

It was the first somebody that I'd spoke to since . . . since I couldn't recall. I didn't want to remember any of it.

"Hello," I said to the cat. "You look more like a dunked rat than a kitty."

She made a cat noise. Very weak. But at least the pair of us were alive, on a tree, and we could see each other. I tried to touch her with my hand and she bited me. Not hard. Yet her fangs were holding to my finger. She licked it, then bited me again.

The wind eased. The rain, however, did not stop. A lighter and softer rain, warmer, and the raindrops hit with a gentle sting.

"Cat, what's your name?"

She didn't answer. Yet her teeth let loose of my finger. Her eyes that had been almost shut closed started to widen, as though she was curious to see who I be.

"I'm Arly."

A large shape, very big, floated near to where the cat and I was clinging. It was a house. Part of it was busted and there weren't any glass in the windows. It made me wonder if any people were inside.

Had the cat lived there?

"Cat, is that your home?"

I figured the cat could swim. Animals usual can.

But I knowed that I couldn't swim a inch. And there was nothing under my feet except one heck of a lot of muddy water. The water was a foamy brown. Everywhere things floated. Parts of houses, sheds, loose planks, oranges, leaves and twigs and scummy dirt. And bodies, bodies, bodies. I saw a dead goat. Later, a black-and-white Holstein cow, with only three legs. One had gotten tore clean off. Even dead bass was floating with their white bellies at the choppy surface. I spotted aplenty of dead catfish.

I begun to notice trees. Not floating, as our cypress still was, but standing and bent. No leaves. The branches were so stripped that the black rain-soaked trunks and twigs looked like a bunch of witches' brooms. The palms were stark bare. Just stalks. Trees without souls. Only wooden trunks of trees that perhaps were wondering if they were dead or alive.

Human bodies floated everywhere.

Dozens of them. More colored people than white.

So many of the bodies were naked. Or close to, as though the anger of the hurricane had intended to strip the living of all leaves and shirts. Not all of the bodies was whole. Arms, legs, and heads was sometimes missing. It was dreadful to see. Hurtful. The small forms of children was saddest.

There wasn't a bit of land.

I could see deep water and shallow water, all of it a dirty muddy brown. Even the foam was browny and sick. I saw tops of cars, black and wet, yet only the tops. No car windows.

No people.

No alive people, only bodies.

It was still raining. Not hard. But it kept coming down. At my chin, the water surface showed the little rings wherever the raindrops would hit.

"Cat," I said to her, "we ought to git to shore, but there ain't a shore to take us."

Still no land. Water blanketed the entire world. It must've looked like this back in the Bible times, the one Brother Smith used to tell Huff Cooter and me. Mr. Noah's flood. I started to wonder how many dead people were around. I don't guess it'd be less than a hundred, and possible more.

"We are lucky, Cat."

She still looked very scared. But, I was knowing, no more frighted than little old Arly Poole.

My foot touched something!

And then my other foot was standing on some solid thing, way below me, beneath all the water.

I prayed it was Florida.

CHAPTER 19

We waited.

For fear of drowning, I couldn't force my hand to turn loose of the tree branch.

My cat friend didn't budge. She remain crouched over her feet, shoulders up in wet points, as though glued to the cypress bark. A wet cat is a very small animal.

"Cat, we're stuck here in a low spot. The water's possible thinner over yonder. But I wonder what's below the surface, down under. It might be a deeper hole."

No sense in leaving hold of a large tree that had floated us through a entire storm. So I stayed, and waited. So did my cat. Cats aren't very tall at all. No cat was about to jump off a safe place and into unknowed water. I decided to let Cat decide for the pair of us. Whenever she left, I could also go.

I final spotted a person, a woman carrying a child and a small dog, wading through water that was above her knees. She plowed through one cautious step at a time. Then another.

"Hello," I hollered.

She didn't seem to hear.

As there was still so much water inside me, I could merely half yell and half cough.

"Hello. Hello."

The woman, I could see as she waded closer, was a large colored lady. Both of her burdens (a dog and a child) was white. All three looked dirty and wet and as tired as I was. The colored lady was searching one way, then another, calling out a name.

"Wilbert."

Again I yelled to her. "Hello. Over here."

She couldn't hear me a bit.

"Wilbert," she kept calling. "Wilbert Day. Where you be, Wilbert honey? Wilbert. Wilbert."

Her voice sounded as if she was crying.

Ripping off a long cypress twig, longer than I was tall, I waved it in the air, back and forth, splashing the water on one side of me and then on the opposite. It made the cat flinch.

"Hello," I kept calling. "Over here."

The hollering, plus the weight and labor of waving my branch to and fro in a half circle, made me real tired. But I didn't quit. I kept it up until the lady noticed me.

She final looked my way. "Wilbert?"

"No, it's me . . . Arly Poole."

"You seen my man, my Wilbert?"

I shook my head.

"He gone," she cried. "Wilbert be clean gone."

The water wasn't as deep now. I could stand without any help. So, it was time to be brave. Or act it. Grabbing a quick but firm hold on my cat, in spite of her hissing that she wanted to stick on the tree, I started wading to where the colored lady was still holding the child and dog.

As I got close, she spoke.

"You a boy."

"Yes'm."

"Who you be?"

"Arly Poole. I'm a sort of a member of The Golden Prophets. You know, it's a church. The Golden Prophets of Salvation."

She just stared and said, "We Baptist."

Wading closer, I said, "You're the first person I seen alive. Everyone else is got drown. Honest."

"It's fearful bad," she said.

"Yes'm. I'm sorry you're missing Wilbert."

"You a polite boy. I can tell you got raised up among a nice family. A proper family."

Remembering my daddy, Dan Poole, a vegetable picker from Shack Row, I said, "Yes'm. My daddy was a rightful proper gentleman."

"What be your name again?"

Near to her now, I said, "Arly Poole."

She shrugged. "I don't know no Poole peoples. Poole? No indeed I don't. You from here in Moore Haven?"

I blinked at the half-dunked cars and washed-away buildings. Nothing looked like anything. "Where we at?" I asked. "Is . . . *this* . . ." I couldn't believe I'd final found . . . *nothing.*

"Maybe it be Moore Haven . . . or close to." She looked around. "But I don't see anyplace I know. Nothing, or nobody." She turned to me. "My name is Hyacinth Day." She almost smiled. "My peoples all call me Hya, like it sound like saying hello."

On all sides of us, as Mrs. Day and I stood in the knee-deep water and mud, there was near to nothing that looked like a town or a city. Moore Haven was mostly two things. Water and busted wood. Floating bits of boards. There was no land. Trees, most of them bare, sprouted up from the shallow water like stakes. A series of large logs, straight up.

Mrs. Day looked confused. "Maybe," she said, "we ain't here."

"I don't understand."

"It sure don't look like no Moore Haven," she said. "Not a bitty grit like the place I got born at. Maybe we be miles away."

Her dog had spotted my cat, and in a breath it was plain to see they wasn't intend to be friends.

"I got a letter," I said, feeling it inside my shirt. "What day is today? I'm supposed to git to Moore Haven before my new family forgits I'm coming."

"It be Sunday . . . Sunday evening."

For some reason I could recall the date . . . 16 September 1928. It was Delilah's birthday.

We met people. Not many. A man, a old woman, and two children. Then a few more people appeared. Everybody asked everyone where we were. Nobody knowed for sure. We all guess. None of us were from the same place.

"There's no water," a woman quietly said. "All this water, and there's no water to drink."

"No food," a man whine. All he wore was a shirt, badly tore, wrapped around his middle and crotch, just enough to cover him decent. Seeing him made me look down at my own clothes. My trousers had only one leg; my shirt only half of one sleeve, and no buttons. Needless to say, no shoes or stockings on me.

Not a one of us was proper dressed, because all of our clothes looked like rags, or less. Rags and string. Whether black or white or in between, we appeared to all be of one color:

Mud.

Everything and everybody had been coated brown.

We all sloshed around in circles, wading in the murky water, seeing that nothing looked like anything we'd ever see before.

My stomach was so empty I was hurting. I had to find something to eat, for myself, for my little wet cat, and for anyone else I could find food for. There didn't seem to be stores, or houses. Just heaps of gray lumber that was twisted and tumbled into scrap.

Mrs. Day nodded at a tree. "Bless me," she said slowly, "but I think I seen a tree like that someplace. It a split oak."

From one of the oak tree's large lower branches hung a rope, frayed and snarled, appearing as if a child's swing had once hung there. Maybe a tire.

I tried to remember Mrs. Newell's cousin. And then did. His name was Alfred Bonner.

But now there was no Moore Haven.

I looked at my soaked unreadable letter, as worthless as I felt.

CHAPTER 20

All night long people cried.

Out yonder in the sawgrass, voices called names, as each survivor was calling the name of another who couldn't be found.

"Louise."

"Jack . . . Jack . . . Jack . . ."

"Shirley May?"

"J.W."

A child's voice kept calling, "Rusty. Here . . . Rusty."

The sawgrass was taller than a man, and razor sharp, and I could hear people scream when cut, or trapped. The vacant building I was trying to sleep in was listing like it was drunk and fixing to fall. Every so often the rafters, slowly drying, would creak in the dark.

I held my cat close, gently stroking her fur to make it fluffy, and telling her that she could stop trembling. She didn't.

It rained.

When morning came, I crawled off the pile of boards I'd slept on, and carried my cat outside. Again, there was no land anywhere, but the water seemed shallower. Only ankle deep.

I saw a long wagon.

Two men were working, loading bodies on the flatbed. For the most part, the dead people were without clothing. One of the men was on his knees, digging another corpse up out of the mucky water and sand. "Oh no," he final said. "It ain't Margaret." Then he looked all around as if his Margaret would appear.

Shovels were scraping.

Anyone who could find a shovel was using it, hoping to find a missing friend or relative. Other men were tearing boards loose from destroyed buildings, for coffin lumber.

Everyone searched for food. Few found it.

Every house had been destroyed. Many a roof had been ripped off; on other houses, the black tarpaper hung down in shreds, tore and twisted. No house was where it had first been built.

I helped a lady dig. We pawed wet mud with our hands. She was very old, quite weak, and kept calling a name. "Loomis . . . Loomis." We never found him, but while I was helping her look, she died. Right there, not ten feet away from me. She lied herself down in the mud and died with her eyes and mouth open.

A lot of the wasted wood was so ruined by the hurricane that the timbers appeared to have got snarled like yarn by a kitten. There weren't enough plank for all the coffins that was needed, so the dead were disposed of another way.

Piles of humanity got doused with coal oil, and then set on fire. Thick black smoke was billowing up from the mounds of cremating bodies. The smell made me gag.

As the water slowly retreated, I found what once

had been a store. The water-rotted food smelled real bad, but it didn't chase me away. Instead, I searched for something to eat, for me and my cat. It was all under some fallen trees, custard apples mostly, and deep in the wet soil. My hands raked the mud like a hungry dog after a buried bone.

I located some canned food.

No labels. They'd washed away for keeps.

Uncaring as to what kind of food I'd find, I busted open a steelplate can by pounding it on the upper edge of a sharp coral rock. It mashed open. The cat was into it fast. Watching her eat made me jealous, almost crazy, so I pulled her away and licked at what she'd been licking.

It was a kind of potted meat.

The cat come back, and we both finished it, without fighting each other.

Can after can I pounded open by the same method. Sweet potatoes, corn, stewed tomato, turnips, and applesauce.

We ate enough. And hid the rest.

Then we slept over the unopened cans, to protect them from the other people. Doing it, I knowed it was wrong, and told myself so, without words. But nobody was going to steal my food. It was *mine!*

Waking up, we ate again. The cat wouldn't leave me. She was smart enough to know that I was warmth and food and safety. And that I petted her. She wouldn't drink the flood water. Not a lap.

As I whacked open another can, white drops of liquid splattered on me. It was canned milk.

"Cat," I said, "Lady Luck is smiling your way, because I don't like this stuff enough to hog all of it."

The cat did.

Right then, I decided on her name, and tried it out

on her, petting her some so she'd stretch out and sleep. "Lady Luck," I called her, because there weren't many a *lady* near Okeechobee that had survive with the good *luck* of my cat. Perhaps she'd shared her luck with me.

More people showed up and held a prayer meeting, thanking God that we'd got spared. We was still alive, above water.

Other people come.

City people, on a bus from Miami.

They didn't come to help. Only to stare at us, and gawk at all our muddy misfortune. They pointed at the stacks of smoldering human bodies and took pictures with a camera machine.

Every day, people in clean clothes come on a bus to look at us. They never brung food, or water, or the medicine stuff that a ample of folks needed. I couldn't believe that all they come for was to sightsee our burning dead.

All of the tourist people wore *shoes.*

I looked for Coo Coo. Nobody ever heard of him. Or of Delilah, or Our Father John, or any of the Sisters. People didn't talk too much. A lot of the folks ducked in and out of the crushed houses, looking for their belongings, or somebody else's to use. People looted such silly stuff. I saw a woman, with hardly any clothes on herself, hurry out of a house with a fancy needlepoint pillow, and a birdcage with no bird inside it. The man with her carried a baseball glove, a fake pinky flamingo, and a cracked mirror. Another toted a clothes tree. But nobody owned any clothes to hang on it.

The Red Cross people come.

They worked really hard, and long hours, to set up canteens and emergency centers, passing out free food, and water you could actual drink. Also some clothing. The Red Cross lady give me a fresh shirt that was too large, but I thanked her anyhow, about ten times. It smelled clean.

I don't guess I can honest say that I'd liked everything the Red Crosserites give me. They stuck a long needle to my arm and squirted some serum into me so's I wouldn't take sick with malaria. So they said. Then, while I was getting over the hurt of that needle, a second Cross lady pumped me another jolt. She said I wouldn't get typhoid fever.

Lady Luck didn't get a needle at all. And, even so, she didn't get sick as I did that night. I didn't know which needle had given me the midnight misery. Next morning, I had me the trots. My backside burned like a smudge pot and I throwed up until I dry heaved. If all this wasn't worse than malaria or typhoid, you'd really have to convince me.

I overheared one of the Red Cross ladies say, "There's no electricity, no telephones, and no plumbing. It's a miracle that the few who are still alive don't go insane."

More rain.

It was near to impossible to find a dry place, so, as a result Lady Luck and I were wet, day after day. Everyone was. The Red Cross people had looked pretty and neat when they'd first arrive. Now, most of them turned as soiled and tired as us rest.

But they almost always brewed hot coffee. It tasted really good, and had a way of making me forget how wet we were.

I didn't get to know anybody's name. People would come to where we were, dig in the mud for their missing relatives, call out names, and getting no answer, then leave. The only friendly face I saw again was my big colored lady who'd saved the white child and white dog,

Hyacinth Day. The dog and child were gone. I hoped they'd both found their families.

She was alone.

"Hello, Mrs. Day," I said.

"Hello."

Made no reason to ask if she'd located Wilbert, her man. Her empty eyes told me no.

"How's your cat?"

"Good. Her name is Lady Luck."

Mrs. Day petted my cat. Then she wrapped her arms around both me and Lady Luck, holding us close to her. She didn't smell bad at all. Only like somebody's mother.

"We have food," I said. "Come on."

Mrs. Day wept.

CHAPTER 21

Tar come to us.

He weren't but maybe five or six years old, and didn't have any family, or food, or any clothes. Naked as a wet crow.

His little body was shiny black because he'd been walking a long time under the rain. Little silver beads of water all over him, top to bottom.

His name, he told Hyacinth and me, was Tar Calhoun.

"Where do you live?" I asked him.

Saying nothing, he just looked around in every direction, and then pointed off to somewhere, as if guessing. Tar Calhoun, however, final mumbled out a name of the place where he'd lived.

"Mo Haven."

From a rag she'd found, Hyacinth was making a long shirt for Tar to cover most of him. So, I went back to the Red Cross canteen place, to beg a drink of water and three doughnuts (for Hyacinth and Tar Calhoun and me) and again I asked them, "Any news about Moore Haven?"

The two Red Cross women looked at each other before answering what I wanted to know.

"We ought to tell him the truth."

"I suppose so. What's your name, son?"

"Arly Poole."

"Arly, it's been reported that there's over a thousand people drowned in Moore Haven. It's right nearby, just north of here a mile. Or rather it used to be. No one can recognize much of anything up there. Plus the National Guard's unearthing more bodies every hour. Before they're through, according to the latest count, the dead may total even two thousand."

"I'm sorry," the other Red Cross lady said.

Returning with the doughnuts, I didn't jump right in and tell my sorry news to Tar. Instead, the three of us ate our doughnuts in silence. I fed part of mine to Lady Luck. So did Tar. It made me like him. Because I figured he was plenty hungry. Everyone was.

I couldn't taste the doughnut. It tasted dead, like Moore Haven and my letter.

We found a dry shed.

Mrs. Hyacinth Day seemed to know what to do, in order to build a shelter for three people and a cat. She built us a bed of boards, covering it with dry rags and weedy grass. The three of us slept together, close as fingers, along with Lady Luck.

Two skinny white men come to our shed one night, looking for food, or liquor. Mainly, as I seen it, in search of trouble. Or lending some to us. They didn't smile.

"What you want?" Hyacinth asked.

"You got any booze, nigger woman?"

"No, I ain't. I'm a Baptist lady."

The two whites shared a dirty joke. "You ain't no lady at all, darky gal. Maybe I'll just take you on and prove you ain't."

I saw Hyacinth reach for a short board. It was

thinner at one end, and that's where she gripped it. As the first man come through our little doorway, or tried to, Hyacinth whacked him so hard that he fell on the spot. He bleated worse than a gassy goat.

"Hey," his friend said, "you ain't got no . . ."

"I got a club," Hyacinth said, raising it up once again, "and I got me a thick arm to swing it." She pointed at the fallen man, who was groaning and holding his head. "Ask him."

"We was just looking for some fun."

"Go way," Hyacinth told him. "Git! I got my two little babies here. Two children and a mean dog that'll capon you with his first bite. So, old mister, if you'd aim to keep whatever you got . . . leave us be."

They left.

"Trash," muttered Hyacinth.

I couldn't say a boo. All I could do was look at Hyacinth Day, in respect, and Tar Calhoun did likewise. As for Lady Luck (our mean dog), whose ears had been throwed back, and spine arched, she turned a couple of circles between Tar and me, curled up in a ball, and slept.

I couldn't sleep.

Hyacinth did. So I stayed awake and whispered to Tar Calhoun, asking him about Moore Haven and what it'd been like. He didn't have too much to say. Tar, I was starting to figure, hadn't strayed very distant from his own dooryard. Not until the hurricane hit. Perhaps it was possible that Tar was the only Calhoun left alive. Maybe, to him, the storm (and what happened afterward) was so dreadful bad that he didn't want to remember one doggone thing.

He stuck closer to Hyacinth than a wart.

If Tar would cry in the night, Hyacinth was holding

him close to her, rocking him, and singing her go-to-sleep song:

My baby. He my baby.
Sleeping soft and soon . . .
Under all the shiny stars,
Underneath the moon.

At night, I'd lie beside Hyacinth, holding the wet pulp of my letter, and thinking about my friend Coo Coo. I certain did miss him. Closing my eyes, I could almost smell him, soil, sweat, and all.

Charles.

I never did know his family name.

Coo Coo was probable dead, I guessed. Not too many people lived through that hurricane, so the story was going. Even though I weren't very practiced at praying, I said more'n one prayer for Coo Coo, hoping he'd stayed alive.

In more than name only, I was starting to feel that Coo Coo be my grandfather.

CHAPTER 22

A hooded truck rolled in.

The truck was painted a greeny brown, the color of a rotten olive. It didn't arrive alone. Two more trucks come too.

"It's the National Guard," somebody said.

The soldiers were real young. Not too many years older than I was, with faces that hadn't much used a razor. They wore big orange boots, wraparound leggings, wing pants, high collars above a row of dull buttons, topped off with what appeared to be half a helmet. One bystander told me their rifles was Springfields.

They marched in lines, arms all swinging, for close to five minutes, as though they was fixing to git our attention. Then they broke ranks, stacked their arms, and smoked. Or chewed.

I didn't know why they'd come, and neither did any of us who stood watching.

"Hyacinth, how come the National Guard's here?"

She shook her head. "Dunno. Keep order maybe."

One olive truck started up its engine, and left, carrying two of the Guardsmen.

Tar and I followed the National Guard as they

marched again, this time without rifles. All a Guardsman carried now was a brown stick. I heard one of the
soldiers call it a riot club. It looked hard enough to
smart. Each Guardsman had a box pack strapped on his
back. When it come time to eat, the soldiers opened the
top flap and pulled out bread slices wrapped in gray
paper, then ate. One of the soldiers wasn't feeling so
hungry so he tossed me his portion. Lady Luck and I
ate it quick.

The Guard put up two tents, poles straight up,
pounded in tent pegs, and tightened all the ropes. The
tents were the same drabby color as the trucks.

Dirty tan.

The Red Crossers come to visit, and talked, pointing at the rest of us plain people without uniforms, and
talked a lot more.

But then the National Guard gold-bar officer came
over, saluted, and said, "Ladies and gentlemen, your
National Guard is reporting here for duty." He laughed.
"I'm not quite certain where *here* exactly is, but here we
are. My name is Lieutenant Field. We're here to protect
you, your children, your livestock, and all property real
or personal, by martial law."

"Soldier boy," said a woman, "we don't got a
anything to steal."

We laughed.

So did the young officer. "I'm just a second lieutenant," he said. "All I do is obey orders. Because if
Captain Blanton tells me to keep order, that is what my
platoon and I do." He saluted once more, smiled, and
left.

I followed, and so did Tar. Noticing us, Lieutenant
Field fished two small pieces of chocolate out of the
breast pocket of his tunic and gave Tar Calhoun and me

a free treat. It was a *wow* thing to eat. "Thank you, sir,"
I said.

"Say, you're a very polite youngster. Do you mind
telling me your name?"

"Arly . . . Arly Poole."

"And *his* name?"

"Oh, this here's Tar. Tar Calhoun. He don't actual
say a awful much, because he got washed here, jaybird
naked, all the way from Moore Haven."

Lieutenant Field stopped smiling. "Just yesterday,"
he told us, "my platoon and I visited Moore Haven. It
is quite near here." He sighed. "Or rather, its remains."
The officer shook his head. "Horrible. I never realized
what a hurricane could do to a little city. It's a bug
beneath a boot."

The officer sat on the truck's tailgate, and then
pulled Tar and me up to sit on either side of him. Tar
Calhoun moved right away quick, so I'd be between him
and the lieutenant.

"I don't bite," Lieutenant Field told Tar.

"He's shy," I then explain. "Leastwise, that's what
Hyacinth usual says. He's not afraid. Only shy."

"Who is Hyacinth?"

"She's . . . well, she's sort of our . . . our mama."

The lieutenant bit his lips.

"Are you boys . . . orphans?"

"No," I said. "Not for sure. I got me a letter, so's
I can go live in Moore Haven."

The officer put a hand on my shoulder.

"Arly, I hate to say this, but somebody ought to
give you the facts. And here they are." He swallowed.
"Hardly anyone is alive in Moore Haven."

"Nobody at all?"

He shook his head. "Very few. It's a nightmare of
wet death. I was here two years ago, in 1926. And it was

dreadful even then. The water in Moore Haven was over ten feet deep, but briefly. And even so, more than a hundred people drowned."

"How come you got saved?"

"I was in Clewiston, southeast of here, when the 1926 hurricane came. It destroyed Miami. I was staying with my mother, father, and sister at the Clewiston Inn, which had recently been built."

I waited for the officer to remember.

"It rained, Arly. Lake Okeechobee was very high, and deeper than safety would allow. I listened to some of the old-timers in Clewiston, men and women who were friends of my parents, tell us about the recent floods."

"What floods?"

"In Moore Haven, only six years ago, the flood waters were knee-deep due to excessive rainfall. That was 1922. The town flooded again in 1923. Nobody seemed to sense that the danger was building. Lake Okeechobee was a overfilled bomb of water, ready to be ignited by a major hurricane. And, as you know, it came."

"I don't understand it all," I said, "or how it sudden come to happen so fast. How did it?"

Lieutenant Field jumped up, fetched a white tin washbasin, filled it at one of the truck's water barrels, and returned to Tar and me.

"Picture this, if you will." He set the basin on the flat tailgate. "Lake Okeechobee, because of years and years of generous rainfall, became a basin full of water. Filled to its brim. In fact, overflowing. So, here comes the hurricane, one of the largest and fiercest ever officially recorded, anywhere. A lot of hurricanes begin near Africa, and I presume ours did too. Now, then, the powerful wind, plus a lot more rainfall that comes along with it, raises the water level here, where we are now, at the southwest bank of Okeechobee."

"What happened?"

"Arly, it's as if a giant hand, or unforeseen force, tilted the basin. That's what a wind storm can do. And over goes the basin, the lake, all over Moore Haven."

Without warning, the officer dumped the basin at me and Tar. We jumped off the tailgate to stay dry.

"Do you understand, Arly? Do you, Tar?"

We nodded.

"Good. Because now, perhaps, you youngsters can explain it all to me. I'm rather unsure. My parents certainly did not raise me to become an atheist. And I am not. Yet, when I surveyed the community that was once Moore Haven, finding naught except need and wreckage and debris, it all made me wonder how a God in Heaven can allow such a tragedy."

Lieutenant Field sadly shook his head.

Tar said nothing. He merely stared at the overturned washbasin that had earlier been filled with water. Then, much to my surprise, Tar said something. "Okeechobee," he said, "dump us a lot mo water'n that."

The officer smiled. "Indeed so."

He jumped to the muddy ground. "Now," he told Tar and me, "I have my duties to perform. And orders to carry out." He knelt down to us, to Tar and me, as though the three of us was comrades. "I'm very grateful," he said, "that the two of you were spared." He grinned. "Who knows? Perhaps old Lake Okeechobee knows enough to spare the best people, because our Florida deserves a tomorrow. A future generation. A few more little Tars and little Arlys."

Lieutenant Field stood up tall. "Arly and Tar, I proudly hail you." He gives us a sharp salute, and then he was inside the truck, barking commands, and was gone.

Tar and I waved goodbye.

CHAPTER 23

The National Guard returned.

Tar Calhoun and I were outside of the shed where we lived with Hyacinth and Lady Luck, and we hooted a hello to the National Guard soldiers. We raced to greet them.

After both of the trucks had stopped, the troops unloaded themselves, and their supplies, and boxes. But no Springfield rifles.

"Arly!"

Hearing my name, I looked at the back of one of the trucks. Someone was being helped to the ground, and it weren't one of the Guardsmen.

"Coo Coo," I said, running to him.

Grinning with every tooth he had (not too many), Coo Coo looked dirtier and happier than I'd ever see him. He held out his arms to me. We sure did hug each other. Right then, I knowed how beautiful a lame old pickie could smell. It was like I was home.

"Arly," he said, "I was afraid you was . . ." He couldn't seem to finish what he was efforting to say.

"I was feared *you* was," I said.

He looked at me. "I'd fell down. Then the Nationals come along, to help me git up. One of them soldier boys, I guess he's a officer, said that there was a kid named Arly over to here. I couldn't believe my ears. But I fibbed and said you was my grandson, because they's trying to put families back together. So I picked you, Arly. You're all I got."

"Coo Coo, I'm so happy you're alive."

"Me too." He looked at Tar. "Hey, who's your little pal? Is this new friend of yourn a boy or a gal?"

"Boy. This is Tar Calhoun. Say hello, Tar."

Tar didn't. All he done was stand there in the long shirtdress that Hyacinth had put him into.

"His mama's coming," Coo Coo said. "That woman don't seem to look like too much pleases her. Certain not me."

"Oh, that's Hyacinth. Her name's Mrs. Day, not Calhoun, and she's sort of a mama to us both. It's like we're a family. And we even got a cat. Her name's Lady Luck." I turned to my small friend. "Come on, Tar. Don't be afraid. Coo Coo's nice, like Hyacinth."

Coo Coo walked in the middle.

He was holding my hand, and Tar's too. We was both hauling him toward Hyacinth, to meet her proper. I could, however, feel that Coo Coo was sort of dragging his feet.

"You seen Our Father, or Delilah, or any of the Golden Prophet Sisters?" I asked Coo Coo.

"No," he said, "I sorry ain't. It's sad."

"We mustn't lose hope, Coo Coo. That's what Hyacinth is always telling Tar and me. Every day, she walks off to places and calls out for Wilbert, her man."

Nearing our shed, the three of us come to where Hyacinth stood waiting. It was plain that she was looking at Coo Coo as if he begged a bath and that the air around him needed a fresh breeze. Earlier, she'd already attacked both Tar and me with one of her treasures. A bar of soap. Hyacinth had even attempted to scrub up Lady Luck, without too much success. Except for hissing.

Hyacinth grunted. "Kids," she muttered without smiling as she eyed Coo Coo. "They's all time tugging home a lot of useless junk."

Tar and I had already heared Hyacinth Day's daily opinion of what she called *trash*. There was black trash and white trash and Mex trash. Like sugar candy, she said, human trash come in all kinds of flavors, and none of it was worth knowing, or keeping.

"This is Coo Coo," I said.

"Maybe so," Hyacinth said in a huff, "and maybe no."

"He's awful nice," I said. "Honest he is. Because his real name is Charles, and he's been baptized."

"You can *forgit that*," Coo Coo spat.

"Tar likes him," I said.

With her fists on her generous hips, Hyacinth looked poor Coo Coo up and down, and made a face at him. "Well," she said, "what Mr. Tar Calhoun cotton to, and what I favor, is plenty different."

"Please like him, Hyacinth. Please do. You just gotta. Coo Coo is . . . well, he's sort of my grandpa."

Hyacinth said, "I wouldn't claim it too loud. On account somebody might hear and believe you."

"Morning," said Coo Coo.

"One more mouth to feed," Hyacinth snorted.

Right then, Lady Luck paraded out of the shed, stretched, arched her back, then sat to lick a paw. Tail up, she stroll over to Coo Coo, sniffed his bare feet, which was their usual color of field dirt, and rubbed her side on his bony white shin.

"See?" I asked Hyacinth.

Coo Coo scratched hisself (a action I'd bet the

world that Hyacinth noticed) and then asked Hyacinth if she was the boss. Even though I holded quiet, I'd come lately to figure out that Hyacinth would act dreadful close to being the boss anywhere she do select.

"Ain't no bosses no more. You a picker?" she asked Coo Coo.

"Used to be, a while ago back. But later, until the hurricane hit us, I was sort of a Prophet."

Hyacinth looked at the dirty knees poking through Coo Coo's sorry trouser legs, with their raggy bottoms. "Don't seem to be much *profit* on *you*."

"Well," said Coo Coo, "before the storm, I got slicked up enough to become a acting honorary of The Golden Prophets of Salvation."

"A honorary *what?*"

"Kind of a honorary . . . performer."

Saying no more, Hyacinth turned and went inside our shed, the little make-up place where the three of us had been living, with Lady Luck. She come back out again, frowned her face, and tossed her precious hunk of brown soap to Coo Coo. He natural dropped it. This seemed to please Hyacinth. She now was wearing a slight smile, for a change, as Coo Coo bent careful to fetch it.

Hyacinth barked a order:

"Wash! If you can remember how."

"Yes'm." Coo Coo looked around in a pitiful way, as if he'd been commanded by devils to do a dishonest deed.

"Come on," I telled Coo Coo. "Keep along with me and we'll find the washing place. Come on now."

Tar come too.

Lady Luck followed us, as though not wanting to miss an event that few eyes had ever seen: Coo Coo's uniting hisself with soapsuds. He didn't smell like a rose. But then, Coo Coo never had. He'd always smelt like a old wino who'd only owned one raggy shirt, which he might lend to somebody worse off.

"You gotta like Hyacinth," I said.

Before answering, Coo Coo stared at the soap in his hand, as if wondering what it was. "I ain't washing to please nobody. Because I'm not fixing to tarry around here, or toe the mark for *that* bossy Queen of Sheba."

"She's in the Bible," I said.

Coo Coo stopped. "Who? That ornery hellion?"

"No. Sheba's in it. Honest, because Our Father John read me about it, how the Queen of Sheba come to visit Solomon." I laughed. "If Hyacinth is Sheba, then I s'pose you can be King Solomon."

"Me? I ain't wise. Not like old Solomon be."

I winked. "You'll be wise to wash."

Coo Coo chuckled.

"Arly, I missed you, boy." Leaning forward, he kissed the top of my head. Falling to his knees on the muddy ground, he put his thin old arms around me. He was shaking. "Oh, I done missed you awful bad."

"I sure missed you, Coo Coo."

"You real did?"

I nodded, wondering how anybody alive could smell so bad, and yet so good. "I'm glad," I said, "that we're pals."

"Aw," he said, "maybe we're even more'n that. If you don't mind at all, I'd like to be your adopted grandpa, for keepers."

Seeing as I'd not never had me a grandfather, or a mother, I said, "I'd like it too."

"Then it's a deal," Coo Coo said.

To seal the bargain, we both pretend to spit on our hands, then shook. His hand felt so hard from field working that it was like holding a eagle claw. Or a tool.

Earlier, Hyacinth had discover a horse barn. No

horses in it. But there was a tin washtub, so old it was turning green. She'd dumped out the muddy storm water, righted it, and let the frequent rain do the rest.

We called it our washing place.

Yet we never was so stupid as to leave our soap there. Had we lost it, Hyacinth might've handed Tar and me some of what she called *correction*.

Coo Coo washed.

Tar washed too.

And then, so did I.

Lady Luck was washing herself, with her tongue, and it was simple to see that she was the cleanest of all. Cleaner than *clean*.

Except for Hyacinth, who'd invented it.

CHAPTER 24

Coo Coo stayed.

But he and Hyacinth Day didn't speak to each other. To know Coo Coo was to understand that the old coot didn't natural take to everybody. He wouldn't cross Hyacinth's path.

Few did.

Most every day or so, Coo Coo would up and disappear, melting away like smoke. He never told any of us that he was going. Coo Coo just plain *git*. Then he'd return at sundown with a burlap bag chock full of produce of one kind or another: tomatoes, cukes, sweet taters, squash, peas, butter beans and shell beans, collard greens, and celery. As much as he could tote.

"Where you finding these eats?" I'd asked.

Coo Coo shrugged. "Ya gotta know where to shop. And how."

One morning, when Tar and Hyacinth was still asleep, I snuck off our bed. Leaving the shed, I went to spy on the close-by place where Coo Coo spent his nights. And some of his days.

Sure enough, out come Coo Coo.

Over his shoulder lay a empty burlap sack, hanging limp and useless. It was early dawn. Not quite enough light to call it morning, but close. Enough dark for me to shadow after the old pickie and not git seen.

Inside a clump of low-grow palmetto, Coo Coo stopped. He skinned out of his shirt. Then he done a strange thing. Leaving his shirt all rolled up in a tight ball, stuffing it under a bush, Coo Coo pulled the burlap bag over his head, poking his skinny arms through two holes, his head through a third.

He wore the burlap sack like a shirt.

I followed him for a mile, I'd guess, and then for another. As I was fixing to give up, because Coo Coo was running away, he passed by a bunch of wrecked vehicles. Cars, buses, and trucks. Some other people were nearby, not doing too much. For some reason, most of the people was wearing burlap-sack shirts, like Coo Coo.

I followed him.

Looking one way, then another, Coo Coo snuck behind a large, long, half-buried truck that was mostly under mud. He disappeared. It was as though he'd found a door to out-of-sight. Moving in closer, I waited.

Coo Coo come back. His burlap shirt was off, and the sack was now bulging with some sort of a cargo.

A cargo that *clinked* as he walked.

"Coo Coo," I said, "what you doing?"

Almost dropping is load, the old picker turned on me, frowned, then hissed a warning like a cornered possum. "Dang you, Arly. You follered me."

"Yes, I did."

"Why? Ain't we pals no more?"

I nodded. "Sure, we're pals. I was just nosey, that's all, to find out what exact you was up to, and where."

Coo Coo pointed a finger at me. "I don't like gitting spied on. No, I don't.

"What's in the sack?"

Coo Coo snarled, "None of your pesky business."

I come closer.

"Well," I said, "it ain't vegetables."

"How do you know?"

I smiled at Coo Coo. "On account," I telled him, "that I never heared no turnip rub another turnip, and go *clink*."

"It ain't the concern of a child."

"I'm not just any child. I'm Arly."

Coo Coo sighed. The burlap sack was heavy, maybe heavier than the old geezer could handle. Coo Coo set it down to haul in a breath. "It's wine."

"Wine?"

He nodded. "Yup." With a toss of his head, he motioned behind him to the secret half-buried truck. "Inside the van, there's a load of wine. Bottles and bottles and bottles full of it. Wine up the geegaw. More'n a army could knock back."

"And you're stealing it?"

"No. I'm only looting a little bit of it."

"Looting is stealing."

"Who said?" Coo Coo asked.

"Hyacinth."

Coo Coo made a disgusting noise. "That old scorpion. She'd disapprove of Tyrus Raymond Cobb stealing second base."

"What are you going to do with all that wine, Coo Coo? If you drink it, all you'll do is make yourself sick, and then you'll puke it up, or wet your trousers."

"What do you care?"

I touched his hand. "Because I do. I'd be a rotten kind of grandson if I let you choose the sorry road. That's what Our Father John used to say . . . that drinking strong spirits only led to sorrowful."

"Holy Joe." Coo Coo spat. "He's probably now

drownded and buried under a ton of mud, yet he still's pestering me to . . . to *reform*."

"You been baptized."

Coo Coo said a awful word.

"Shame," I said. "Now what would Hyacinth say if she could hear you speak such?"

He said worse.

"Coo Coo, how come you want to act like trash?"

He sighed. "Maybe I am."

"No," I said, "you ain't never. Because there's so much more inside you than . . . than *wine*."

"Arly boy, a sip of wine don't about to hurt me that smart."

"Did you actual say a *sip*?"

"Maybe two sips." He laughed.

I laughed too. As I done so, I was recalling something that Our Father John had told me, about people. It was late one night, the Sisters was all asleep, and Coo Coo had somewhere located a bottle, and was ripening as mellow as a midnight mule.

"Arly," said Our Father, "if we profess to be Christians, then we must learn that there's something more important than converting people."

"What's that?" I'd asked him.

Our Father John had smiled. "Understanding," he said. "Our dear old friend Coo Coo partakes of wine, and then makes himself ill, but you and I must understand *why*. Perhaps we ought to accept Mr. Coo Coo as he is. Thus, our gift to him . . . is a gift of . . . Acceptance."

Standing there, looking at Coo Coo and a burlap sack loaded with looted wine, I knowed only one thing. That I'd accept Coo Coo as he was, not as I wanted him to be. Because, he happen to be pretty doggone good,

135

as far as I could see, and it was near enough perfect for me.

He bent over.

"Arly," he said, "I don't fix to drink all this wine. Oh, to be straight out, maybe a bottle. I'm aiming to trade it for eats. Produce. For me and you and Tar Calhoun." Coo Coo made a sour face. "Even for the Queen of Sheba Hyacinth Day." He smiled. "I'll trade most of it for food."

His smile sort of blossomed among the wrinkles. Nobody, not even a saint or a devil, could ever actual dislike Coo Coo for a entire day. It weren't possible.

As he looked into my face, I could see that he'd always be a friend. A pal. Yes, a grandfather. He would be Coo Coo forever, and not change. A changing of some of him might mean I'd want to change all, and I certain didn't. There was no way I'd cotton to wipe out any of the good inside him, in order to scrub away a few dirty specks of bad.

I waited.

Coo Coo limped away to barter the wine bottles for some vegetables. This time it was a sack of sweet corn. On ears.

Later, little Tar and I and Coo Coo shucked it. Hyacinth boiled it in a pot she'd found, and it was golden good. Coo Coo smiled at Tar and me as we ate. As he tried so hard to gnaw the yellow kernels off a cob, using so few teeth, I had to salute Coo Coo.

In the only way he could, he hunted for us.

CHAPTER 25

Again it rained.

"I about feel," Mrs. Hyacinth Day said, "that I'm to turn myself to a fish."

The National Guard come, and went. All was good folks, yet we all knowed that none of them would be staying. They wouldn't be keeping friends.

Coo Coo stayed.

So did I, and Tar, and Hyacinth Day. Plus our cat, Lady Luck. To those around us, we five must've appeared to be a odd-looking family. Yet we were one. We'd become *one* thing. All together, Hyacinth, our Baptist, recited a Holy Bible piece. She called it a verse. It was about *atonement*. Yet she told us it was a big word in three parts:

At-one-ment.

According to Hyacinth Day, this all meant that it was our whole group that honest mattered, not just a one person here, or a one over there. What counted was *us* together.

As the days grinded along, one at a time, I started to remember who I was, that I was actual a boy named Arly Poole.

I recalled Jailtown.

In my mind I could see the Lucky Leg Social Palace, and the giant pink leg on its roof, that served as its sign, its come-on. Remembering, I wondered who would still be alive in Jailtown. I prayed that Essie May Cooter would live, even though a part of her must've died when she made her deciding to go work at the Lucky Leg, for Miss Angel Free.

The Red Cross people had a radio.

There weren't no electricity juice, so that meant their radio had to run on a battery. But it ran. The static cracked and cracked something dreadful, yet we managed to hear the news, from Miami: "Moore Haven has located close to two thousand dead bodies," so the radio man said. "Each day," he'd gone on to tell us, "the National Guard is finding more victims. No one knows their names." He paused. "The dead cannot identify the dead."

There was more news to hear: "Jailtown, a smaller community to the north, on the western bank of Lake Okeechobee, suffered almost as severe a death toll." "Over a hundred citizens fell to the flood, as a direct result of the hurricane."

I wondered about all of the people I once knowed, such as my teacher, Miss Binnie Hoe. And the generous lady at the boarding house, Mrs. Newell.

On certain days, the Red Crosser's radio recited the names of the dead people in Jailtown. I listened up sharp for people in Shack Row.

Sometimes I'd hear names that caused my mouth to drop open . . . like Mr. and Mrs. Dinker Witt. And a Harly Yoobank. And the judge, Jailor Jim Tinner, who'd be missed by few, as he'd lived most of his life in old Captain Tant's back pocket, right alongside of his snot rag.

"Judge Tinner," the radio voice said, "had prac-

138

ticed law in Jailtown for over forty years, a leading citizen of the community, and one who'd be sincerely mourned."

It made me smirk to hear such a lie.

Captain Genesis Tant, and his field boss, Roscoe Broda, along with Judge Tinner probable done in pickers and cane choppers by the hundreds.

Thinking about whether or not Miss Hoe was really dead, one more body buried under the acres and acres of mud, or swept away out into the miles of sawgrass, got me down.

"Miss Hoe," I said, "you almost changed my life."

Right now, here where I was living, or trying to, there weren't nobody that I could talk to about the only schoolteacher that I'd ever met. A little bird of a woman with a heart of a giant. It was strange how Miss Liddy Tant, the Captain's daughter, had brung her to Jailtown, to begin a school in a empty store. Our school, however, had burnt up. To ashes! People claimed arson. But that sadness hadn't drain no spirit out of Miss Binnie Hoe. She paid a call on Miss Tant, who owned the Jailtown lumberyard, and asked her to donate some boards for a new school.

Brother Smith had builded it. We all helped.

Our new school was tiny, for certain, but we had our school, on safe land, at a place where big Brother Smith could keep a eye on it, and keep it from a torching.

As I thought about it all, both the good and the sorry, I was poking around in a mud bank, finding firewood to lug back to Hyacinth.

Coo Coo come along.

"Arly, what you up to?"

"Searching, that's all."

"For what?"

"I don't actual know. Maybe I can stumble on something to better us. Could be a chair, or a table. Even if it's only a cookpot. Hyacinth can put it to work, making a meal."

Coo Coo sighed. "Lately," he said, "I been starting to think that it takes about all the hustle we got, just to near starve."

"But we're alive."

"Almost."

I smiled. "It beats picking."

Coo Coo laughed. "I'd have to honest admit that about everything beats kneeling in the dirt, under sun, to yank up a carrot."

"We got away, Coo Coo."

He nodded.

"Hey," I said, "we both actual run away to freedom, and we won't have to load ourselfs into that old blue bus no longer."

I heared a car horn.

Lifting my head in the direction of the sudden sound, I saw a black motorcar. It was inching toward us, again blowing its beep-beepy horn in order to scatter a few gray chickens that was pecking at bugs in the road. Plain to see that the driver didn't try to run over a chicken. Some folks do.

In the front seat was two ladies. Looking closer, I couldn't rightful believe what I was seeing. Rubbing my eyes, I took a second glance. I'd seen this car before. But where?

The car stopped.

A side door swinged open, and somebody I knowed stepped out onto the wet dirt. She wore a real pretty dress that was trimmed with white lace. And wearing shoes.

"Miss Liddy Tant," I said.

140

Coo Coo gulped. "You *know* that there woman?"

"Yes, she's from Jailtown."

When a second person slowly exited from the black car, I near about fainted. It was my schoolteacher.

Miss Hoe.

My feet couldn't move. It was like the mud had stuck me in the roadway, and wouldn't turn me loose. I felt my mouth opening. Nothing come out. And nothing seemed to be coming in either, because I couldn't breathe.

Coo Coo didn't say a word.

He just turned and run off at a quick limp.

"Arly?"

It was Miss Hoe's voice. Had I been dead for a hundred years, I'd know her little sparrow voice and its cheerful chirp.

Then I was running to her.

She hugged me like I was clean. "Oh," she keeped on saying over and over. "Oh, my Arly Poole."

"I was so afraid you was dead, Miss Hoe."

"No, I somehow survived that hurricane, as I did the ones that cursed us in 1926 and 1910." She stepped back to study me. "I'm so thankful you're safe."

Miss Liddy stood by, in her usual quiet way, just being Captain Tant's pale skinny daughter.

I spoke to her real respectful. "Hello, Miss Tant. I'm glad you're safe too."

"Thank you, Arly."

"You've grown," Miss Hoe said.

"Have I honest?"

She nodded. "At least an inch by eye's measure." Then she felt my shoulder. "But, oh my, you're so thin."

Right then, I wanted to tell Miss Hoe and Miss Liddy Tant that there's no such animal as a chubby picker. Yet I holded it all back inside me, on account these two ladies had never spent even a day harvesting beans. Maybe to them, the vegetables somehow all growed at the grocer.

"Who was that elderly man?" Miss Hoe asked.

"Oh, that's Coo Coo."

"A friend of yours, no doubt."

"Yes'm. A lot more besides. He's become family. Off away somewheres, Coo Coo's got hisself a real grandson, but he lost his picture. And worse, he can't remember the name."

Miss Hoe sighed.

"So much sadness," she said. But then her face brightened, as she touched my hand. "And yet, so much joy."

Reaching inside my shirt, I pulled out my letter. It was in bad shape. Not even a Miss Hoe could read a word of it.

"What is that?" Miss Hoe asked me. She didn't seem to know what it was.

"My letter," I told her. "You said not to lose it, so I keept it close. I'm sorry it got so . . . so messy."

Her hands held my shoulders.

"Arly Poole, did you actually guard that letter for an entire year, through everything you've had to endure?"

I nodded, and tried to smile.

"I don't guess I guarded it good. But I lost Brother Smith's Bible and I done likewise to *Tom Sawyer*. I'm real sorry. All I could keep was my letter."

"You did splendidly," Miss Hoe said. "But I fear that Mrs. Newell has lost her cousin. Mr. and Mrs. Bonner have not been found. I predict they're both dead."

It hurt to hear it. What my teacher was telling me

was that I wouldn't be going to a new home in Moore Haven. I wouldn't get no home at all.

My body started to shake.

"There, there now," said Miss Hoe, holding me close to her. "Don't you fret, Arly. You'll be taken care of."

"Honest?"

She nodded. "I promise you."

"Miss Hoe, I got sorry news. Brother Smith got drown in Okeechobee, with me, when his sculler boat got swamped."

Miss Hoe smiled.

"Arly, I have happy news for you."

"You do? Please tell me, on account I sure could use a portion."

"Brother Smith is alive."

CHAPTER 26

There was room in Miss Tant's car.

I couldn't believe everything was happening so fast. But it was. Right now. This was my first ride in a fancy motorcar, and a lot different than a old blue picker bus.

Miss Tant sat behind the wheel, to drive. I was sitting in between Miss Tant and Miss Hoe. In the backseat rode Coo Coo and Hyacinth and Tar and Lady Luck.

Earlier, I saw that Coo Coo was near shy as Tar. Hyacinth Day wasn't, because she'd probable spit in a gator's eye, reach down his throat, grab his tail, and yank him inside out.

We was on our way to Jailtown.

"I can't believe Brother Smith's alive," I said to my former teacher, and it felt so happy to say it.

"Very much so."

"Is your daddy all right?" I asked Miss Liddy.

"Captain Tant is elderly, and quite ill," she answered. "At present, I am making all decisions regarding our business enterprises, and our family."

We talked more, up front.

In the back, however, nobody as much as said *boo*.

Hyacinth just rode along, with Tar Calhoun asleep on her lap. Coo Coo weren't doing a thing except holding Lady Luck.

As for me, I was wondering what these two ladies intended to do with all five of us. One thing sure. I didn't want to live again in Shack Row.

"Miss Hoe," I said to her, "I'm not ever going back to the Shack Row place. Because if so, please ask Miss Liddy to stop the car so I can scoot."

The teacher patted my knee. "No need. Shack Row was almost entirely washed away by the hurricane. Washed away forever. Miss Tant," she then explained, "intends to rebuild Jailtown. A large and successful sugar corporation is rather interested in the community, and more, it's willing to contribute to Jailtown's future and betterment. Miss Tant is an astute business person and has been making many changes."

"What's a . . . a corporation?"

Miss Tant answered. "A company. Just a fancy uppity way to say company, that's all."

"Jailtown will become a decent place to live, for all our citizens," Miss Hoe said. "Isn't that so, Miss Tant?"

"Yes," Miss Liddy said proudly, "and with a new name someday. A name we can all boast with pride and promise."

Miss Hoe patted my knee.

"You're coming home, Arly," she said, "to a new town that you, and everyone in this car, can help reform."

"Home." I said. "Home, home, home."

Miss Hoe smiled at me. "Isn't that a nice word?"

I nodded. "It's the best. And what makes it so good isn't because it's a place. It's a bunch of people."

We rode for a while, quite slow, because the road was a sorrowful muddy mess. Through the car's window glass, nothing looked familiar. We went driving by a whole bunch of houses that the hurricane had uprooted and set down somewhere else. Junk and loose boards were lying everywhere. Somebody guessed it was Moore Haven, yet nobody knowed for certain.

After we'd passed by a dead cow still half-buried in muck, Miss Liddy had to stop the car. For a moment, she merely sat behind the wheel, her thin white fingers covering her eyes.

She final spoke to Miss Hoe. "We Floridians," she softly said, "are hardy folk. And now we must become even more resolute, in order to find one another, dry ourselves off, and rebuild."

That there was the most I'd ever heard Miss Liddy Tant say. A regular sermon.

For years, I'd always heared about how Miss Liddy had got treated by her father, Captain Genesis Tant. A long while ago, a young gentleman wanted to marry her. But, it was claimed, some of the Captain's men took him in a boat out over Lake Okeechobee, late one night. He never returned.

The local story in Jailtown was this: Miss Liddy and her daddy lived in the same house, yet she and the Captain never spoke another word to each other. Least-wise, so their servants reported, in whispers.

I looked at Miss Hoe. "How come you happen to find me today? Was you and Miss Liddy out for a motorcar ride?"

Miss Hoe laughed. "We have been searching for you, Arly Poole, ever since poor Brother Smith returned heartsick the next morning, to report you missing."

"You been looking all this time?"

"Yes, we have. Miss Tant has driven countless miles. Verna Newell, whenever she could steal a few hours away from the boarding house, and I hiked in circles around Jailtown. First in one direction and then in another, calling your name. We both called out *Arly* until our voices were spent."

I smiled. "Thanks. I was all right."

"What have you been doing for a year?"

"Mostly picking. Coo Coo and I run away from Mr. Boss. We was sort of prisoners on a field crew. But one night it rained really hard, so Coo Coo and me . . ."

"Coo Coo and I," Miss Hoe corrected.

"Coo Coo and I escape in the night."

"How did you live, or eat?"

"We joined a Revival group. The Golden Prophets of Salvation. The leader was Our Father John. All the rest were Sisters. And then Coo Coo and I become stars of the show."

"A tent show?"

"Yes'm. A religious service. You'd be surprised how many people turned up to point at us and laugh. But then a good portion of them wound up becoming Saved. They'd come to jeer, Our Father said, but stay to cheer."

"Weren't no Baptist," said Hyacinth from her back-seat.

"Which denomination was it?" Miss Hoe asked me.

"Uh, as I remember, Our Father John Patrick Mulligan founded his own church. He made it all up hisself."

"Just like," said Coo Coo, "he made up his title."

For some reason, Coo Coo's first remark set Miss Binnie Hoe and Miss Liddy Tant to laughing. A look passed between them.

We rode for a while. Nobody talked much.

Miss Liddy final said something, and it was important. "I do hope," she said, "that my Ford can make it back to Jailtown."

"Is there something wrong with the engine?" Miss Hoe asked.

"No. But we're low on gasoline."

"Are we close?"

"Oh, perhaps within a mile. Riding on *empty*."

Miss Tant and Miss Hoe discussed our mileage while I listened, noticing that the two nice ladies was no longer calling each other by Miss Hoe or Miss Tant. They was formal only for the benefit of the rest of us. Between themselves, they used their first names. Binnie and Liddy.

"There are people up ahead," Miss Tant said.

"Quite a crowd," my teacher agreed.

Riding closer, we could see a group of city people and their camera machines, making pictures of a very large pink object that was partly buried in a high dune of mucky sand and loose junk.

It sudden hit what the thing was. Something that I'd looked at my entire life in Jailtown. Strange, but it was the first thing I'd seen since the hurricane that I recognized right off quick. Instead of high up on a roof, standing up, it was laying on its side, bruised and defeated. Without remembering my manners, I sort of blurted it out:

"It's the *leg!*"

Miss Tant and Miss Hoe didn't say a word.

Their silence, however, was telling me that I'd spoke out too loud, and mentioned something that nice ladies didn't talk about. Leastwise, certain not in public.

Yet there it lay, the giant pink leg that had always been the high-uppest article in all of Jailtown. Higher than the courthouse steeple. The leg. The shapely lady's leg and its red garter and fishnet ropes that was added to look like a fancy stocking . . . the sign above the Lucky Leg Social Palace.

Without a word, Miss Liddy motored her Ford car right on by, and appeared not to notice. Neither did Miss Hoe.

Coo Coo, on the other hand, couldn't hold in his appreciation, as we passed by the famous lady's limb.

"Holy bananas, she musta been a high stepper."

CHAPTER 27

O ur engine quit.
"I'm sorry," said Miss Tant.
"Are we out of fuel?" Miss Hoe asked her.
"Yes, I fear we are."

Miss Tant's fingertip tapped the little round gasoline gauge on the control board. The arrow was pointed to E.

"Empty," said Miss Hoe.

One by one, we piled out of the Ford.

Coo Coo made a gentleman's effort to assist Hyacinth, whose generous size wasn't designed for climbing in or out of a snug fit.

"Leave me be," said Hyacinth. But then, as Coo Coo continued to help her to stand, Mrs. Hyacinth Day had a sudden warming of heart. "Thank you, mister."

Something bad happened. In order to unsqueeze Hyacinth from the backseat, Coo Coo had let loose of our cat. Right then, the Ford chugged a small explosion.

Lady Luck took off running.

Tar and I ran after her, calling her name, but Lady Luck weren't in no mood to stop, at least not until she'd run out of sight.

"Where she go?" Tar asked.

I pointed. "Ahead," I said, "that there is Jailtown. I'd know it upside down."

Beyond some windwhipped trees, I recognized the tower of the sugarcane crusher. High up, and rusty brown. In the past, I'd worked at it when Roscoe Broda dragged me there by a rope.

We run, Tar and I.

Calling out Lady Luck's name, Tar Calhoun and I poked through the bushy weeds and the many piles of loose gray boards. Then we saw Lady Luck ahead of us, a ways off, hightailing toward the cane-chopper buildings.

"Lady Luck," I was yelling. "Come on, Tar. We got to catch her before she's clean gone."

A few poor-dressed people was outside a shack, trying to nail a board into place, whacking it with a mallet. They stared silent at Tar and me when we went charging by, after the cat.

We run through a small shed that was still standing, without half of its roof, and into the open again. Coming to the main crusher, we darted inside. It was darker than out in the sunlight, and I couldn't see much right away. But I could hear a engine. It sounded to me like a truck. But it wasn't. As my eyes got used to less light, I saw what it was, just as the dogs barked.

It was a blue bus! There was only three fenders on it. The left front fender was missing. Beyond the cracked window panes, several scared faces looked out at me. All children.

As three dogs come at us, two men followed behind, both toting guns. Tar was clinging to me, afraid, as the dogs crowded us against a inside wooden wall. All I could do was see those dreadful teeth and hear their growling.

151

"Hey," the taller of the two men said, pointing a finger at me, "I just bet I seen you before, boy."

I knowed his voice.

Mr. Boss.

"You a runaway," the shorter man said. His dogs had Tar Calhoun crying, and me so scared I couldn't even wiggle a toe. My feet seemed to die. Grabbing ahold of my shirt, yanking it loose, he squinted at my chest. "Well, well, well," he said, "looky what we got here. A work number. In code. You owe me money, skinny boy. A chasing fee."

"Where's the old guy?" the shorter man asked me. As he spoke, I remembered his name. Herman, the dog man.

Mr. Boss put a hand to my chest, and didn't do it too gentle. "I feel all them scars, boy. You is branded to me for life. All you got's a number now. And that's all you'll ever have until you die a old pickie, out in the produce field."

The dogs was jumping up, snapping at Tar Calhoun and me, until Herman kicked one of the dogs. It yelped. But then all three turned quiet.

"Where be old Coo Coo?"

"Yeah, he run too. Where's he at?"

Mr. Boss cuffed my face. Both ways, a lot of times. Forward. Back. Forward. Back. His long arm was swinging at me, slapping one side of my face, then the other. One slap cracked my ear and I heared a loud ringing.

"Where's Coo Coo?"

Herman grabbed Tar. "Hey, little bug-eye nigger. I bet you'll know where old Coo Coo's hiding. Where? Tell me. Tell."

As I was holding Tar, with my arm around to protect him, I could feel his body shaking. Tar, who

152

was always so afraid of everyone he didn't know, was now closing in on crazy. His fingers clawed at me like he'd fell in deep water.

Herman slapped Tar. Awful hard.

"Cut out yo circus, boy. Or else I'll maybe let these dogs bite into you so fierce that they'll have you for supper."

Again he hit Tar. Blood spattered on my face.

"Leave him be," I said. "Please."

"Oh," said Mr. Boss, "we catch ourselfs a uppity boy, right here. A nigger lover." His hand grabbed my throat. "You a nigger lover, white boy? Zat what you be?"

"You best tell us right quick," Herman said, "where that old Mr. Coo Coo be hid, or they's won't be a inch of hide on either you."

Mr. Boss and Herman were hitting me again. Harder now. And cuffing Tar Calhoun. "Tell. Tell us. Where's that Coo Coo be? Tell." My lips was cut and I could taste the sweet blood in my mouth, sticky hot.

"Hold it!"

I heard a voice.

It weren't Mr. Boss or Herman.

"You leave 'em go, you hear? Back off. You leave them childrens alone. So back off, mister, and *now*."

Holding to Tar, I looked to where the voice was coming from, and saw. There, walking toward all of us really fast was three men. All very big. Two dredgers, men who worked the big machines that scooped dirt from the ditches. I could tell by their boots. Both of them white men. Between the two whites come a very big colored man, with white hair. I knowed who.

It was Brother. His deep voice spoke again, even though one of Herman's dogs was snarling in his throat.

I wanted to say "Brother Smith," but my mouth weren't able to form any words. Or any name.

"Turn those two childrens loose," Brother said. His voice wasn't ornery or angry. It was steady and deep, like it was leaping right out of the Bible.

"We got guns," said Mr. Boss. "All we doing is taking what be our property. All legal. Capturing a couple of runaway field hands that owe us money."

"Yeah," said Herman, "these are runaways."

Brother's big voice boomed out.

"They . . . be . . . *children*."

"We got more men outside," said one of the large dredgers. "Some of us are missing our kin."

Hurrying to the blue bus, the other dredger looked in its door. "There's more kids in here. A lot more. Maybe nine or ten of 'em. Good grief, they're tied up in ropes."

"They all pickers," said Herman.

"That's correct," said Mr. Boss. "Pickies, every one. They all been tagged legal."

"And branded," said the dredger at the bus. "I can smell the stink of burnt flesh."

CHAPTER 28

A gun clicked.

Eyes closed, I holded Tar.

Listening, as I lay on the damp ground, against a wall, I could hear more voices. More dredgers were coming. To me, it sounded close to half a dozen men. Some were calling out the names of their missing children.

Out of one swollen eye, I could see that the dredgers carried a knife or two, but mostly ax handles and long shovels.

"Arly? Arly?"

The voice I heared weren't Brother's.

It was Coo Coo.

He must've run all the way, chasing after Tar and me. Because he was so sudden there. Without looking, I could almost smell Coo Coo, the way my nose remember my father.

"I'm here," I called out to Coo Coo.

He was close.

"Arly . . . Tar . . . you all right?" He panted for a few breaths. "It's me, your crazy Coo Coo friend. And you both be safe."

A fight started.

One of the dredgers, from what little I could hear, found his missing daughter inside the blue bus. I couldn't listen to all that got shouted, by both sides, yet I could hear enough to know that the dredgers were using their shovels and their ax handles to beat on Mr. Boss and Herman. And their dogs.

The noise growed awful bad.

Then guns. A woman screamed.

I don't know who fired the first shot. But, to me, it sounded like a shotgun blast. The guns kept shooting. Coo Coo was bending down, on one knee, above both Tar and me. I could smell him and hear him.

"Keep low," Coo Coo said.

As the guns continued, Coo Coo stayed to shield us, hovering over Tar and me like a mother bird on a nest. We crouched under his wings.

I heared a man yelp.

And a dog.

Then . . . WHAM . . . another shotgun.

"Harry? My God, they killed Harold."

More noise. The strong stink of exploded gunpowder was in my nose with every breath, forcing me to hold the air inside me, trying not to breathe at all.

"Do him, Burton."

"Get him!"

"Watch out, Louis. Louis?"

"Harry's fixing to bleed to death, Thurman."

WHAM. WHAM.

"I'll learn you dang slavers not to hogtie a bunch of kids. I'll learn you good and proper."

I could hear the ax handles and the shovels being used against Herman and Mr. Boss. Again, a dog whined, but then was still.

WHAM.

Another gun.

Coo Coo stiffened, and tried to speak.

The place was filled with dust, shouting and swearing, plus the smell of gunpowder. So bad that I didn't want to see or listen.

Coo Coo said my name. "Arly." But, because so much else was going on, I couldn't catch whatever else he was saying. Then I felt him slump onto Tar and me, and I could feel Coo Coo's shaking.

"Coo Coo?"

He answered, but very weakly.

"Hey . . . Coo Coo . . . you all right?"

He weren't.

Tar knowed it too. "Coo Coo dead," he said.

"No!"

"Coo Coo be dead, Arly. Shooted."

With my hand on Coo Coo's chest, I pressed it against the tired old body. He was bones and leathery skin and little else. For a second or two I thought I'd felt a heartbeat. But then nothing. No throb at all.

Coo Coo didn't move.

"He dead, Arly. Coo Coo be gone."

Tar was right.

The back of Coo Coo's raggy shirt was drippy wet with blood. Warm and sticky. I said his name as though I'd not expect a answer. None come.

The noise stopped.

Yet I couldn't stop saying "Coo Coo . . . Coo Coo."

Now the men were talking, instead of yelling, or fighting. It all sort of sudden quit. Somebody was close to us. A big person; but, because of the dust, I couldn't actual tell which one.

Then I saw him for certain.

"Brother Smith," I said. "Brother."

Blinking, he slowly looked our way. He didn't

know Coo Coo, or Tar. Right now, my face was so swollen that he probable didn't know me either, not by sight.

"Brother Smith . . . it's me . . . Arly."

He bended down to feel Coo Coo, soon knowing he was dead, and moved Coo Coo's body. Then he put a big arm around me, and around Tar, to hold us gentle.

"Arly . . . Poole?"

"Yes."

"You . . . your face . . ."

"Mr. Boss beated me bad. He hitted Tar and me." Though I couldn't steady myself to quit shaking, I pointed to my friend. "This here is Tar Calhoun."

Brother Smith closed his eyes, as if saying a very quiet and private prayer to God. "Arly . . . you is alive?"

I nodded. That was about all I could do, because it hurted my mouth to move it. It felt like I had apples under my lips. All I could taste was blood.

"Arly Poole, I thought you be drown."

"No."

"That night on Okeechobee. Wind and all. My sculler boat fill up and flip over. I push a oar under you. That's all. I sink deep, then come up and hit my head on the boat. It was upside down, so I hook a arm around a seat board. There be some air inside. Not much air. Enough to keep alive on. Until the breeze blowed me to shore."

Reaching out, I touched Brother's hand.

"You alive, Arly." Brother Smith smiled. "Oh, I got to tell Missy Hoe and Mrs. Newell. I'll tell about you to Missy Liddy herself. You alive! Arly Poole be alive."

Tar stayed close to me.

To him, because he was so small, and scared,

Brother Smith must've looked like a thundering mountain.

Brother took Tar's hand. "You be all right now, little one. Don't you cry. The mean people is dead. Along with their killer dogs."

"Coo Coo be dead too," Tar said.

"He needs burying," said Brother. "And we ought to bury Mr. Harold and anybody else who dead. We bury the bad ones as well as the good."

We did that, in groups.

As we all come out of the cane crusher building, Miss Hoe and Miss Liddy Tant come hurrying along. Behind them, carrying Lady Luck, come Hyacinth, about as fast as such a large lady could move.

Miss Liddy couldn't quite look at me.

Miss Hoe did. "Arly," she said, pulling out a clean white hanky to gently blot the blood off my face. "Oh, my little Arly Poole."

Hyacinth worked on Tar, and in her care he final settle his crying to a few silent sobs. Brother Smith just stood there, holding Coo Coo in his mighty arms, as though the old picker be a busted rag doll.

"Arly," he said, "where you want to rest your friend?"

For a minute, I couldn't quite think of the right place. But then it come to me. A plot nearby.

We brung a shovel. Tar Calhoun and I took turns to dig a grave beside the flat grave of my father, behind what little was left of our shack, in Shack Row. That's where I wanted Coo Coo to rest.

Beside my daddy.

"Proverbs . . . And thy foot shall not stumble. Yea, thou shalt lie down, and thy sleep shall be sweet. Amen."

Without my asking, Brother Smith had spoke his

Bible words in a proper way that only Brother Smith could do. Before we covered Coo Coo, I lay down to put both my arms around his neck, feeling his scratchy white beard stubble against my face. To inhale all of his gritty goodness inside me. To keep.

"Coo Coo," I whispered to his ear, "thank you for saving Tar and me. I guess I'm the luckiest boy in the world."

With a shovel, we covered him over and pounded the sand into a tidy mound. There he lay, next to another picker, Mr. Dan Poole. Someday, I'd lie here too.

We all stood silent at Coo Coo's grave. Miss Tant, Miss Hoe, Brother Smith, Tar, and Hyacinth holding Lady Luck, and me. My entire family. My home.

Brother lightly touched my shoulder. "Arly, how did you say this gentleman's name go? I forget."

"Charles," I said. "His name is Mr. Charles Poole."

Brother Smith nodded. "He a kin to you?"

Standing up straight and proud as I knowed how, I told a big lie, one that only God would welcome, in Acceptance.

"He's my grandfather."

DATE DUE

NOV 0 2 2005			
NOV 0 6 2005			
GAYLORD			PRINTED IN U.S.A